THE HAMBURG SWITCH

Angus Ross

THE HAMBURG SWITCH

 WALKER AND COMPANY • NEW YORK

First published in the United States of America
in 1980 by the Walker Publishing Company, Inc.

ISBN: 0-8027-5418-X

Library of Congress Catalog Card Number: 79-48051

Printed in the United States of America

10 9 8 7 6 5 4 3 2 1

This one is for Iwan and Inga

Foreword

'How did the course go?' Charlie asked.

'It damn near killed me,' I said. 'I'm getting too old for that sort of rhubarb.'

'Bloody give over,' he said, 'McVicar can give you a good couple of years.'

'He's used to it,' I said. 'Besides, the bastard's not human.'

'How about the rest? Improve your German, did you?'

'What do you think?' I said. 'Five hours a day, seven days a week – '

'You ought to be grateful,' he said, 'for a whole month in sunny Sutherland.'

'Look, you can keep it,' I said. 'That house is a bloody mausoleum.'

'Miss the booze, did you?' he said. 'All that clean living a shock to the system?'

'All right, Charlie,' I said, 'now tell me what it was all in aid of.'

'Jagersberg,' he said. 'Professor Eberhard Jagersberg.'

'Who's he when he's at home?'

'Head of Physics at the Doppler Institute.'

'That's in East Berlin.'

'I know it's not in Heckmondwike, Farrow – do we *have* to put up with these dogs?'

'They live here, Charlie.'

'Live here? They act like they own the place. Anyway, friend Jagersberg wants out.'

'Do we want him then?'

5

'Everybody wants him. He's so far ahead in laser research, he's practically out of sight. He's the reason we're losing satellites.'

'What satellites – who's "we"?'

'NASA have lost three probes in five months, quite unaccountably. They were all in firmly established orbits, and – '

'Just a minute,' I said. 'You mean they were got at by laser?'

'That's right, Farrow,' he said. 'Don't ask me how, because nobody knows . . . none of our lot, that is. We think Professor Jagersberg knows, though.'

'You keep saying "we", Chas,' I said, 'but if it's NASA that's losing the hardware, why can't the Yanks get him out?'

'They bloodywell would, given half a chance. That's why we've got to move fast.'

'How fast can you move on those crutches, Charlie?'

'You've noticed them, have you?' he said.

'It's only five weeks since you copped it. That damned slug nearly took off your leg.'

'Thanks for reminding me, Farrow. I'm touched by your tender concern.'

'Don't get me wrong – I'm concerned about *me*. These little jaunts of ours have a sickening habit of turning nasty. That bloody Congleton lark just about did for both of us.'

'You scared I might slow you down?'

'For Christ's sake be reasonable, Charlie.'

'Relax. I'm not going with you,' he said. 'You've been promoted. You're in charge.'

'In charge of what?' I said.

'Getting Jagersberg home and dry.'

'I know – I mean, me and whose army?'

'You and Mackenzie,' he said.

'*Mackenzie!*'

6

'What's wrong with Mackenzie?'

'He's still wet behind the ears!'

'You'll just have to watch him then, won't you?'

'Yes, and who the hell's going to watch me?'

'Stop whining, you'll get local help. We've a Resident out there, codename Pablo.'

'Where's he live?'

'East Berlin, of course. Don't worry, he's been there a very long time, and he's highly organized. You'll contact him through our man in Hamburg, old Percy Harvester.'

'It sounds like a sticky one, Charlie.'

'That's why the Man's sending you.'

'Yeah, I know, I'm expendable.'

'We all are, Farrow,' he said, 'it's the nature of the business – look, call off this damned hound.'

'He likes you, Charlie.'

'Bloody dog hairs . . .'

'Come here, Jake,' I said.

'Now the other bugger's started!'

'You too, Sam,' I said. 'Come on – into the kitchen.'

'While you're there, make some tea.' Then, 'Didn't you hear me?'

'Yes, I heard you. I've put the kettle on. So when does this little shindig get lift-off?'

'Tomorrow morning,' he said, 'the Leeds–Bradford airport at half past nine.'

'We're travelling by 125? Christ, it must be important!'

'You'd better believe it,' he said. 'If you make a balls of this one, Farrow – '

'Do leave off, Charlie,' I said. 'What'll you do – slap my wrist or something?'

'That kettle boiling yet?'

'In a minute. Listen, if we do pull this one off, it won't half annoy our American cousins.'

'Bugger the cousins,' he said, 'you just get Jagersberg

out of there, and after that who cares? Let the fat-arsed diplomats sort it all out.'

'That's what pisses me off. In the end they'll probably give old Jagersberg to the cousins, anyway. So why not let them get him out?'

'Ours is not to reason why.'

'Jesus, you can say *that* again. I sometimes wonder, that's all.'

'Look – are we having some tea, or aren't we?'

'Coming up, Charlie,' I said.

Thursday

'The minicab's 'ere, Mr Farrer.'

It sounded as though Mrs Tidy, the ancient but in-defatigable lady who 'did' for me two afternoons each week, was calling from the foot of the stairs. I answered to let her know that I'd heard.

'All right, Mrs Tidy – be down in a minute.'

I was sitting on the edge of the bed with my raincoat on and my suitcase already packed, looking down at the .357 Smith & Wesson magnum cradled in the palm of my hand. Sorely tempted to take it with me. But against my instinct, and my better judgment, discipline prevailed. Charlie had made a point of reminding me of the Man's inflexible attitude towards the use of firearms abroad, and in language somewhat forceful. I sighed and got up off the bed and returned the Smith to its hidey-hole. Then I picked up my bag, and after one last look around the bedroom, turned and went downstairs. Mrs Tidy was in the kitchen, mopping paw-marks off the tiled floor.

'Well, I'll get away then, Mrs Tidy. Thanks for doing the dogs. If you run out of tins for them, just get some more at the shop and charge them to my account. Is there anything else you'll be needing?'

'No, I don't think so,' she said, 'you get off, Mr Farrer – about a week, did you say?'

'Give or take a day or two, yes.'

I looked past her, through the kitchen window. The labradors were out in the wilderness garden, doing the round of smells they had smelled a hundred times before.

An exercise which seemed never to pall, in spite of its unvarying routine. First Jake would sniff and then, when he was satisfied, lift a proprietary leg. His brother Sam would stand in line, patiently waiting his turn in an order of precedence never disputed. I was mildly startled, as I watched the performance, to find myself wondering if I might ever see it again. That the thought had manifested itself annoyed me, and I thrust it from my mind. Such notions were most unprofessional. Mrs Tidy was watching me, her shrewd old eyes bright as new black buttons.

'You all right, Mr Farrer?'

'Er, yes, Mrs Tidy,' I said. 'Well, I'll be off, then.'

' 'Ave a good trip.'

'Thanks. See you next week,' I said.

The minicab driver looked up from his copy of *The Sun* as he heard the front door slam, and climbed out of the car to take my bag. He stowed it in the boot, and I got in front beside him.

'Yeadon, Squire?'

'That's right.' I looked at my watch. 'You've got sixty-eight minutes.'

'Tons of time,' he said.

Ripon was just beginning to stir. We cut swiftly through the narrow streets of the old town and were soon well out on the Harrogate road. Traffic was light. We turned right at Killinghall to cut across the Skipton road and pass the army camp before hitting the rolling country beyond. The road snaked over the hills to drop down and bridge the Wharfe at Poole. A long steep drag up Poole Bank, and then we were speeding out along The Top with the airport tower in sight. As we swung left along the narrow approach road, my watch said twenty past nine and I paid the cab off a few minutes later.

'You timed that well, lad,' I said.

The young driver grinned. 'Not hardly,' he said, 'the next flight's not until ten.'

10

I added a tip. 'Don't take bets on that.'

'Beg pardon?'

I picked up my bag and stepped into the little concourse. Mackenzie was waiting for me. He saw me enter, and hurried forward.

'Good to see you, sir,' he said.

I shook his hand, then shook my head as he tried to take my bag. 'How do, Mackenzie,' I said, 'and listen – let's start as we mean to go on. My name isn't Sir, it's Farrow, and if you think for one moment that I'm not fit enough to carry my own small suitcase, you should never have taken this job.'

He flushed. 'I was just – '

'That's all right. Where's Harvey?'

'He's waiting out in the kite. He's had a word with Customs, I think we can go straight through.'

The two bored Customs officers looked up as we passed, and followed our progress with curious stares. Wondering, no doubt, what it was that made us special. They made no move to intercept us, and Mackenzie led on through Gate Two. I followed him out on to the grey, windswept tarmac and almost stopped and blinked. I had been expecting to see the eager shape of the Section's neat little Hawker Siddeley 125, but someone, and almost certainly without consulting the poor old taxpayer, had decided to trade it in for a new model. The gleaming white-and-brown HS 700B standing out on the apron looked absolutely brand new. The short sleek fuselage and the Garrett TFE 731 fanjet engine pods which snuggled against it port and starboard were cheated out in orange and yellow trim which ran on up the high dorsal fin, and the cabin mask, underbelly, and stubby swept-back mainplanes were finished in a rich chocolate colour. An overall effect which was very striking indeed. It was a truly beautiful aeroplane, but beauty, I knew, was not at all its function. Its function was to fulfil, and when necessary even exceed, performance specifications probably unequalled and certainly unsurpassed by any non-military aircraft of its size anywhere in the world.

That section of the fuselage just aft of the flight deck which formed the boarding steps was lowered to the ground, and as we approached, Sam Harvey ducked out. Although he had been the Section's pilot for all of the dozen years I had worked for the Man, Sam still looked and acted like a kid just out of school. Same gangling gait, same tousled fair hair, and same effervescent humour. But something different, now, about the grin. That broken front tooth had been capped with porcelain. He aimed a mock-punch at my guts.

'How are you, Marcus, you sad old bugger?'

'Bearing up,' I said. 'You've been to the dentist, sunshine.'

'All the better to pull the birds.'

'And got yourself a new toy, I see.'

'Not bad, is she?' he said.

'Too bloody good for the likes of you.'

'Haven't you heard? I passed my test. The L-plates were causing too much drag.'

'Yes, well, let's get on board, before you forget all I taught you.'

'You want to take her up?'

'No fear. You've probably broken something, and just want to shift the blame.'

'Christ, foiled again!'

Mackenzie cleared his throat. 'I think we ought to be going, Mr Farrow . . .'

'You heard the lad,' I said.

'Don't be so bloody conscientious, Jock.'

'All right, Sam,' I said, 'let's go.'

The cabin layout was opulent. Armchair comfort for eight, and three of the port-side seats formed a couch

12

which might easily be used as a bed. The mod cons included flush-toilet and washroom, a dinky carry-on bar, and a well-stocked refreshment unit.

'Not bad, eh?' said Sam.

'Very swish – got my bumf?'

'Not this time, young Jock must have it – how's old Charlie, by the way?'

'He's still on crutches.'

'Is his tongue still on crutches?'

'What do you think?' I said.

'Hey, that reminds me: there was this Irish toast-master – '

'Later, Sam,' I said. 'Let's get airborne, so that young Mackenzie can stop consulting his watch.'

'Roger – oh, there's just one thing more. For Christ's sake, don't mess up the carpets. If you *must* be sick, use the bags.'

'Get knotted. Listen, I was flying off ships when you were – '

'Yes, I know, you've told me before. When I was a scheme in my daddy's skull.'

He turned away, laughing, and passed through the bulkhead door which closed off the cabin from the crew-seat and flight-deck. Less than a minute later we heard the starters whine, and the fanjets picked up with scarcely a tremor. As Harvey ran through his checks, Mackenzie produced a bulky buff envelope and handed it over to me. I tore off the flap and spilled out the contents. The passport was three years old, and genuine in every respect except for my name and occupation. For the purpose of this little jaunt I was, it seemed, a travelling salesman whose name was Herbert Stroud. I counted the sheaf of used German Deutschmarks. Five hundred. Just over a hundred pounds. Which, in Hamburg, would go roughly nowhere. But there were two Eurocredit cards, so the miserable sods in Section accounts might therefore be circumvented. As I began to read the single sheet of typewritten notes which accompanied the bumf, there was a hissing rush of hydraulics as Sam released his brakes, and the 700B began to roll. We taxied smoothly out to the runway, and the powerful little jet was up and away in next to no time at all.

The briefing, which told me virtually nothing I didn't already know, was headed *Read and Destroy*. I tore the paper into tiny scraps and flushed them down the toilet, and it seemed that I had barely returned to my seat before we were circling Hamburg's Fulsbüttel airport.

The time was ten minutes past ten.

Percy Harvester's office in the consulate at Hamburg was quite definitely bigger than my larder back at the old farmhouse, but Harvester was a very large man and he seemed to fill it by himself. He must have topped three hundred pounds, a Robert Morley-like character with dewlaps under his chins. Most of his remaining hair consisted of eyebrows which beetled over small deep-set eyes of a pale hard blue placed close together on either side of a hooked beak of nose. His bulk was swathed in a wrinkled lightweight suit of an indeterminate muddy brown, and the collar of his shirt looked slightly grubby, as though on its second day. His fruity voice matched his old-school tie. He had chubby baby's hands, which he kept laid flat on the doodle-covered blotter on top of his black metal desk. The whisper was that in his youth Percy Harvester had been a very hard man, but his vague bland manner belied the legend. Appearances can deceive.

'Did you have a good flight?'

'Very smooth,' I said.

'Are you settled in at the Schloss Hotel?'

'Yes. We registered en route.'

'Don't eat there, whatever you do. The food's appalling, y'know.' I shifted on the plain wooden chair, and my knees hit the front of his desk. Mackenzie stood at my side, by the door, shoulder blades against the wall and arms folded across his wide chest. Harvester glanced up at him. 'Shall I ask them to bring in a pew?'

There would hardly have been room for one. 'No, thank you, sir,' Mackenzie said. 'Really, I'd much rather stand.'

Harvester switched his pale gaze back to me. 'I gather, Farrow,' he said, 'that you're quite familiar with Lübeck-Travemunde.'

'Who told you that?' I said.

'You spent six months there in '45. 807 Squadron – correct?'

'That's right. We flew off *Vengeance* into the ex-Luftwaffe airstrip at a place called Blankensee.'

'Quite. It's one of the reasons that you were picked for this job.'

'It's a damn poor reason, then. I haven't been to Lübeck in well over thirty years. Anyway, what's this caper got to do with Lübeck?'

'Everything,' Harvester said. 'We've chosen Travemunde as the ideal spot into which to welcome friend Jagersberg.'

'We? Who's we?' I said.

'Yes, all in good time. First things first, as they say. I take it you've never met codename Pablo?'

'Not to my knowledge,' I said.

'Well, you'll meet him on Saturday.'

'Where?'

'In East Berlin. Do you like football?'

'*Real* football, yes. If you mean soccer, no.'

He chuckled, shaking purple-veined jowls, then opened a drawer in his desk to fish out a small white envelope and slid it across to me.

'The East Germans don't know rugby league, I'm

afraid.' He really *had* studied my file. 'There's a ticket to Saturday's match between East Berlin and Leipzig. But you needn't follow the play. Just talk to the man in the seat on your left.'

'Pablo?'

'None other,' he said.

'What then?'

'Have patience, Farrow. Pablo will tell you what then.'

'And Mackenzie?'

'Mackenzie stays here – or, rather, in Travemunde.'

'Doing what?' I said.

'Supervising arrangements on this side, dear boy.'

'What arrangements? With whom?'

'With a man called Willi Fischer.'

'Is Fischer one of ours?'

'In a way. He's a freelance.'

'Jesus!' I said, 'that's all we bloodywell need!'

Harvester looked pained at my language. 'I say, steady on,' he said. 'Fischer's most reliable. We've used him several times.'

'I don't give a monkey's left tit,' I said, 'you can keep your sodding freelances.'

'But we *need* this one, Farrow,' he said. 'Fischer's lived in Lübeck most of his life, and he knows the channel up there. We must have someone with good local knowledge. Those defences, you see – '

'All right.'

' – are very damned sophisticated. Fischer has studied them well. You might say they're his speciality.'

'How many men's he got out?'

'Well, actually, Jagersberg will be the first.'

'So he's had no experience, then.'

'No one's had any experience.'

'Well, why pick Travemunde at all? Why not go for one of the Wall routes?'

'You have answered your own question, Farrow. It's

16

because there has never been an escape up there that Travemunde was chosen, you see. In any event, Berlin's no good. Jagersberg is much too closely watched in the city.'

'Isn't he guarded in the country, as well?'

'Yes, but not to the same extent. He owns a small cottage up in Schonberg, goes there most weekends. However, Pablo will brief you in that respect.'

'There's some little comfort,' I said. 'We don't seem to be getting very far here.'

'My dear Farrow,' Harvester said. He folded his hands across his vast belly, 'you must appreciate that *my* role is primarily one of liaison. There is no need for me to know the finer points of detail.'

Which, I had to admit, was normal practice and fair enough.

'All right, then,' I said, 'when and where do we meet this bloke Fischer?'

'I rather thought,' Harvester said, 'you might want to go up tomorrow. Take a good look around. Mackenzie's booked in at the Maritim.'

'Is he, now?' I said. We were talking about Mackenzie as though he wasn't there. As, indeed, he might not have been. He had not uttered a word since declining the offer of something to sit on. That boy knew his place, and I found myself hoping he knew his business every bit as well, Because if he didn't, I could be in trouble. 'Where's the Maritim?'

'In Travemunde, right on the point. It's a fairly new hotel – new since you were there, anyway. I think you will find the place ideally situated.'

'Jolly good,' I said. 'So what do we do in the meantime?'

'Why not just relax?' he said. 'See Hamburg. It's an attractive city.'

'Tell me something,' I said, 'what's the drill for crossing the *Deutsche Republik*?'

'There is no drill,' he said, 'you simply buy a ticket here, get yourself on to the train, and sit tight until you reach Am Zoo station.'

'And once in West Berlin?'

'You cross at Checkpoint Charlie – but you'll see when you get there,' he said.

'Sounds quite simple. If it's all that easy – '

'Oh, please don't misunderstand. You will find the checks rigorous, to say the least.'

To say the least was right. But that was something I learned only later.'

'So when I arrive there,' I said, 'how do I get to the football ground?'

'You should have no trouble at all. The stadium is not very far from the station. You might even find a cab. Any other questions?'

'Yes. How do we contact Fischer tomorrow?'

'You don't. He will contact you. Take lunch at the Maritim Hotel, and Fischer will make himself known.'

'That would seem to be it, then.'

'You have my number, you can always reach me via here. Should you need anything – '

'We'll let you know.'

'Splendid.' He did not get up, but leaned forward as far as his girth would permit and held out his fat, dimpled hand. The strength in his fingers was quite surprising. 'We shall meet again, I hope.'

I hoped so, too. Most fervently.

'Thanks for your help,' I said.

'Now then, Mackenzie, name your poison.'

'I'll get them, sir,' he said.

'You will if you call me sir just once more. What's it going to be?'

'I'd like a Martini and soda, please.'

'Christ, Mackenzie,' I said, 'that's not a drink, that's a woman's drink.'

'I rather like it,' he said.

'Well, there's no accounting for taste.' I turned to the barman again, and reverted to German. 'Do you have Glenmorangie malt whisky?' He seemed very proud that he *did*. 'Good. One large Glenmorangie, and one large Martini with ice, and a twist of lemon, and soda – that all right for you, Jock?'

'Thank you, yes, that's fine,' said Mackenzie.

'How much, barman?' I said.

'Eleven marks fifty, please, sir.'

'Good God! That's just on three quid!'

I had spoken in English. The barman looked puzzled. '*Bitte, mein Herr?*' he said.

'Oh, Christ, never mind. Here, keep the change.'

We carried our drinks to a window table in the near-deserted bar which stood cheek-by-jowl with the Schloss Hotel's grill room. The hotel, although second-rate, was extremely well placed on the Alsterufer, overlooking the huge blue lake around which the handsome city is built. It was a beautiful sunny day, with just enough breeze to fill the sails of the many graceful yachts which tacked to and fro across the wide waters and heaved on the rolling wakes of the long low plastic-topped sightseeing boats.

'Cheers, er . . .' Mackenzie said.

'Sup it slowly. Make it last.' I watered my liquid gold, and took a pull at its peaty delight. 'Ah, that's better. Cheers,' I said.

He watched me pack and light a pipe. 'If we'd travelled commercially,' he said, 'we could have brought in some duty-free stuff.'

'Good solid thinking,' I said, and instantly regretted it. He coloured up like a girl, and I hurried on to make

19

amends. 'Tell me, though,' I went on, 'what do you think of it so far?'

He shrugged. 'It's difficult to say.'

His accent was upper-class Edinburgh. Measured, and very clear. I judged him to be about twenty-four. He had reddish-blond wavy hair, and the good strong regular features of your typical lowland Scot. His skin had the look of being freshly scrubbed, and his teeth were very white. He was two or three inches over six foot, which made him as tall as me, but his lithe frame was not so heavily covered. He would weigh about two hundred pounds against my two hundred and thirty-two. He had to be faster, though. Charlie reckoned he could handle himself. Well, we would probably see.

'Come on, you must have formed *some* opinion.'

'Well . . . it all seems somewhat vague.'

'It won't be when we've seen Fischer and Pablo – at least, I hope not,' I said.

'Do we know who this Pablo chap is?'

'No, and it's better that way. What we don't know can't harm him.'

'I see. You mean if we're – '

' – caught? That's exactly what I mean. Drink up, I could do with some grub.'

'Don't you want another Glenmorangie?'

'Yes, I do,' I said, 'but not at these bloody prices.'

'Force yourself. This one's on me.'

'I think you're a dark horse, Mackenzie. You're leading me into bad ways.'

'Of course, if you'd really rather not . . .'

'All right, go on then,' I said.

He summoned the waiter and gave the order. His German was very good. In fact, it sounded perfect.

'You bilingual?' I said.

'Er, yes, as a matter of fact, I am.'

20

'Well, that's something,' I said. 'You might come in useful after all.'

That made him blush again, but he grinned and nodded. 'I've every intention. Don't worry, I shan't let you down.'

'That's the spirit. Here's tae us.'

'Are you bilingual too?'

'Comes from having Scottish forbears.'

'*Slainte* – wha's like us?' he said.

'Damn' few – an' they're a' deid!' I responded.

He laughed. 'Spoken like a native,' he said.

We lunched in the baroque dining room. Old Percy Harvester had been quite right, the food was pretty poor, but my head was so full of thoughts of the job that I didn't really care. The assignment had taken on a bad odour. Charlie wouldn't have liked it at all. His hatred of working with freelance help exceeded that of my own. Mackenzie seemed to sense my mood. We ate the indifferent meal in almost total silence and when the reckoning came I had it put on Mackenzie's bill. Which made a pleasant change. The parsimonious creeps in Accounts could bicker with somebody else.

I turned our afternoon walkabout of the Free and Hanseatic City of Hamburg into a sort of exercise for Mackenzie, one in which he was to follow me at a short distance in order to spot any tail. It was not that I had any cause at all to suspect that the job was blown at this early stage. My main intention was to avoid the flaunting of our togetherness any more than was strictly necessary, and there was also the fact that I was disinclined that day to make idle conversation. I wanted to be alone with my thoughts.

I left the Schloss by its big main entrance, waited for a gap in the endless procession of gleaming Mercedes, and then nipped smartly across the Alsterufer to head for the beautifully kept gardens of the lakeside Alster Park.

21

Beyond the little dinghy marina, with its orderly ranks of tarp-wrapped boats, a white-hulled sightseeing boat was discharging its cargo of rubbernecks. Most were Japanese, cameras ever at the ready, all spectacles and teeth. I walked along the neat concrete jetty and mingled with them in the small dockside café, where they hissed around buying picture postcards. I bought myself a beer, and took it outside to sit on one of the wooden benches looking out across the lake. The two-mile dog-leg of dappled blue water sparkled under the sun, alive with traffic both sail and diesel. Although at the heart of a bustling centre of commerce, the scene had that holiday air of determined gaiety and carefree leisure. Which did not impinge upon me. I stared across at Hohenfelde, sipping my seventy-pence beer and wishing I were back home in Yorkshire. Yes, albeit painting the house.

Then I remembered Mackenzie. I retraced my steps through the park and crossed the neck of the Aussenalster by the busy Kennedybrücke to turn left into Glockengiesserwall, the magnificent wide thoroughfare which runs through the heart of downtown Hamburg. The fine broad pavements, fronting shops whose windows were crammed with luxury goodies of every conceivable kind, teemed with well-dressed strollers. In a tiny tree-shaded square a makeshift bandstand had been erected, and a very Teutonic brass band was making sentimental music. Fat children licked ice-cream cones, and a clown-costumed man was selling balloons. I passed the carnival scene and meandered through the happy crowds, up towards the Hauptbahnof, the huge and handsome main railway station. When I reached the Deichtorplatz, I turned right along the Ost-West-strasse to parallel the Elbe. Here, pedestrian traffic thinned out dramatically, and a breeze from off the river was almost chilly. Over to my right loomed the extraordinary pile of Chile House, a multi-storey edifice constructed in dull red brick and shaped like a great ocean liner. Towering sharp-pointed prow, and flaring lines port and starboard. Iron rails along its high brick decks. A marvel of fanciful architecture, but soberly practical, too.

I tramped on, with no idea as to whether or not Mackenzie was still with me. I had not looked back to check. My thoughts were now proccupied with the ironies of war. The last time I had seen Hamburg, in 1945, it was nothing but a vast sprawling heap of rubble. Its inhabitants lived underground, in what remained of the cellars. Misery everywhere. A terrible numbing atmosphere of utter, crushing defeat. The people suffered enormously. There was very little food, and decent women were selling themselves for a bar of chocolate or soap. Their deutschmark being literally worthless, all and any items of value – watches, cameras, jewellery, and even fountain pens – were bartered on the black-and-only market for English cigarettes, the universal currency. Life was a constant weary struggle, a grim and traumatic experience for vanquished and victor alike. It had seemed at the time that the ruined city would never rise again.

But now, thirty-four years later, Hamburg was metamorphosized. A truly splendid metropolis. That its citizens were rich was evident in every aspect. I though of Bradford and Leeds, and found the comparisons sadly depressing. Something at home had gone wrong, and the men responsible for the decline had much to answer for. If the Herrenvolk were laughing at us, we had only ourselves to blame.

These were my almost-subconscious musings as I plodded stolidly on. Ost-West-strasse is almost two miles long. I paused when I reached the end to look at my little street-plan, turned right at the Holstenwall, and walked by the side of the Gross Wallanlagen – yet another lovely park – at the top of which looms the great Hall of Justice. When I reached the Gorch-Fock-Wall I had almost completed the seven-mile walk all around the centre of town. Stephans-platz was thronged with people and to get away from the crowds I ducked down a pleasant little side-street towards the Mittelweg, only five hundred yards from the Alsterufer. By this time I was somewhat footsore, and when I spotted a bar I succumbed to the lure of a frost-beaded beer. The entrance was below street level, down a flight of railed-off steps, and the narrow, long interior was attractively dim and cool. I walked the length of the polished bar down to its furthermost end, and sat at a table against the wall. The striking girl who appeared had a smile which evoked long-gone memories of fräuleins and made me yearn to be young. She took my order for a bottle of *pils* and then, as she turned away, I sighed at her fine undulating haunches as she sashayed back to the bar. A well-dressed man at a nearby table intercepted my glance, and made a small moué of sympathy before applying himself once again to the much more attainable business at hand. He· was eating an afternoon snack, plying his knife and fork with gusto and all but smacking his lips.

The humble, underrated herring is one of my favourite fish. I like them plain grilled with lemon and salt, boned and rolled in oatmeal and crisp-fried in butter, soused and served with mustard sauce, and perhaps most of all as your real oak-smoked kipper. But the Germans have a method of preparing herring which we English just don't know. They have the fresh raw appearance of *matjes* but they are not pickled in brine, nor do they taste of vinegar. The texture is that of our finest smoked salmon and to me, now a firm *aficionado*, the flavour is equally good.

When the waitress returned with my fifteen-bob beer, I asked for a plate of the fish. She was back in a flash with the eating irons and a couple of table mats and a big soft paper napkin. Two minutes later, the fish. Served with paper-thin rings of fresh onion and a bowl of soft white rolls and a little dish of knobs of butter. As I set about the snack, I was conscious of someone entering the place. I glanced up towards the door in time to see Mackenzie climb up on a stool at the bar. He did not look, but I knew he had seen me. I heard him ask for a beer, took a sip of my own, and went back to my muttons.

I ate a couple of rolls with my herring, ordered a second *pils*, and smoked a pipe as I drank it. The splendid lass brought my bill, and watched me wince as I checked the total. I added a ten per cent tip and paid and left Mackenzie draining the last of his beer. Outside, I paused at the top of the steps before crossing the narrow street and heading downhill towards the Alsterufer. Straight back then to the Schloss, and as I asked at the desk for my key Mackenzie followed me in and hurried to join me in the lift. A stout matron laden with shopping bags got out at the second floor, and then we had the lift to ourselves.

'Well, what's the verdict?' I said.

Mackenzie grinned and shook his head. 'Negative. Clean all the way.'

'Enjoy your little stroll?'

'Stroll! It was more like a marathon.'

'Do you good, lad,' I said. 'Set you up to appreciate your dinner.'

'You've had yours, haven't you?' he said.

'Hell, no, that was only an appetizer.'

'What time shall we eat, then?' he said.

As we quit the lift, I looked at my watch. 'Make it seven-thirty,' I said. 'I'm going to put my feet up.'

'Want me to give you a buzz?'

'No, I'll meet you down in the lobby. We'll go out for a meal, okay?'

'You're the boss.'

'Right. See you later.'

As I stepped into the room my eyes fell at once on Harvester. He was sitting in the bedside chair, his vast bulk bulging out over the sides. He waved as I closed the door, and watched me shrug out of my raincoat.

'How did *you* get in here?' I said.

A question so stupid he didn't even answer.

'I bring news for you, Farrow,' he said. 'Someone else is sniffing around Jagersberg.'

'Someone like who?' I said.

'That's just it – we don't know,' he replied.

'The cousins?'

'Could be,' he said.

'Christ, can't we find out?'

'We're trying, Farrow.'

'How? Who's "we"?' I said.

'West Berlin's crawling with doubles and triples. We do have our sources, you know. Our people are keeping their ears to the ground.'

'God Almighty,' I said, 'this bloody job gets worse by the minute. It's a right mare's nest from the start.'

I took the shoes off my aching feet and stretched out on top of the bed. Harvester hitched his chair round to face me.

'Come now, Farrow,' he said, 'this isn't the north of England. You're not on your own home ground. You're going to need all the help we can give you.'

'So you keep saying,' I said, 'and I don't entirely disagree. But listen – there's help, and *help*, and the kind you get from double agents is the kind I can do without. I don't trust the devious bastards. They're in this game just for the brass, and the side which pays least is the side which gets shit on, and knowing those twats in Accounts affords me no comfort whatsoever.'

'Point taken, Farrow,' he said. 'But don't teach your grandmother how to suck eggs.'

Curiously, Harvester's huge body seemed suddenly to shed its flab, and I caught a glimpse of the hard man inside it.

'Look, I don't want to argue,' I said. 'Just so you know where I stand.'

'You stand where we all stand,' he told me, 'and you won't be given any information which hasn't been thoroughly checked.' He grasped the chair arms with both pudgy hands and hauled himself up on his feet and lumbered around the bed to the door. 'That's it, then. I'll be in touch.'

'Yes, all right.'

With Harvester gone, I closed my eyes for a nap. But, just for once, sleep evaded me. So I got up and did a Charlie. I soaked in a long, hot bath, and washed my hair and had a shave. By the time I was dressed again, it was almost time to meet Mackenzie. I went downstairs to the bar and recklessly ordered a large Glenmorangie. That was the mood I was in. Mackenzie joined me a few minutes later.

'I thought I might find you here.'

'You were right, then. What are you having?'

'Martini and soda, please.'

'Jesus.'

When we had finished our drinks we went out and found a quiet little restaurant off the Mittelweg. I fancied the pork chops and sauerkraut and a half of decent hock, but settled instead for a stein of ale. Mackenzie had a steak, and asked for a glass of the house's red plonk. Then both of us opted for cheese, and – the hell with it – I ordered a Hine with my coffee.

'What about you, Jock?' I said.

'No thanks, I don't drink the strong stuff.'

'You want to start, then,' I said, 'or you might grow up like Charlie McGowan.'

He chuckled. 'I could do worse.'

'Yes, but you'd have to try very damned hard.'

'I thought he was your friend?'

'What the hell gave you that idea?'

27

'Well, one doesn't always choose one's friends simply for what they are. It's possible to like some people in spite of their little ways.'

I thought about it. He had a point. 'All right, Oscar,' I said, 'never mind the aphorisms – where's your credit card?'

'Lost yours, have you?'

'Don't be cheeky. What d'you want to do tonight?'

'I've been waiting for you to tell me.'

'No, come on, what do you fancy?'

'I somehow don't think you'd approve.'

'You might be surprised. Just try me.'

'If you'd really like to know, I wouldn't mind going to the ballet.'

'The *which*?'

'What did I tell you?' he said.

'You serious, Mackenzie?'

'Perfectly.'

'Count me out, then,' I said.

'But oughtn't we to stick together?'

'I don't see why,' I said. 'Unless you're scared you might get mugged.'

'No, it's just that I thought – '

'Relax, lad,' I told him. 'Fill your boots. You heard what old Harvester said. We've got the night off – remember?'

'What will you do, then?'

'You mind your business, I'll mind mine.' I said it with a leer.

'Like that, is it?'

'You never know, do you? Hamburg's a naughty town.'

When we parted outside the restaurant I walked along to Dammtor S-bahn and caught a surface train to Stern-schanze, next station along the line. There, I changed to the underground and rode the track to St Pauli, at the

28

start of the Reeperbahn, and joined the scattering of Reeper Creepers on what is supposed to be the wickedest street in Europe. I stayed on the right-hand side, and strolled eastwards along its three-quarter-mile length. An endless blaze of flashing neon signs turned the night into day with light more blinding than that of the sun. No one accosted me, and I saw nothing really sinister. I passed several good-sized hotels, all of which looked quite respectable. Two large cinemas were showing bland American films, and the net-curtained restaurants looked discreetly *chic* and, of course, expensive. On a boarded-up building site, night workers toiled under brilliant arc-lamps. An old lady walked a dog with an inexhaustible bladder. There were not many people about, but half past nine was perhaps a shade early. I was working up quite a thirst, but the bars on the Reeperbahn proper put me off my beer. One I ventured into – and out of – was just like a furniture store. Chairs and sofas and ormolu tables of varying periods and styles arranged as though on display at Harrods. Perched on high stools at the bar was a bevy of stunning young lovelies, all beautifully gowned, and looking like a million dollars. Each. I beat a hasty retreat, and turned off into the next side-street I came to.

And this, as they say, was where it was at. I hadn't walked ten yards when a kid with the face of a Boticelli cherub and the figure of a Hollywood star greeted me like a long-lost lover. When I smiled and shook my head, she reeled off a list of curious delights.

'Sounds wonderful, Fräulein,' I said, 'but not just now. The night's too young.'

She shrugged and turned aside to resume her vigil from a sex-shop doorway. The merchandise offered for sale, much of it somewhat larger than life-size, left nothing to the imagination. As I moved away, a youth with pimples invited me to a real live action show.

Alternatively, a deep-blue movie. I declined his offers, too, and paused in front of a newsagent's window. The glossy magazines on display had positively riveting covers. As I studied one weird gymnastic arrangement, I felt a soft hand on my arm. A whiff of some aphrodisiacal unguent. She was almost as tall as me. A stunning, statuesque redhead wearing a knee-length blond mink coat. As I turned my head, she held the coat open. All she had on underneath was a sort of topless black lace bra, a wisp of garter belt and long, long suspenders to hold up her stockings. Thighs like an Arab mare. She struck a pose in the light from the window. A genuine redhead, all right, and never was I more sorely tempted.

'Do you like it, darling?' she said.

A heavy English accent.

'Like it? I love it,' I said. 'But I can't afford it, sweetheart.'

'Oh, Christ, you're English,' she said. Birmingham, possibly Wolverhampton. She couldn't have been more than nineteen. The smile left her face and she closed her coat and looked me up and down as though I'd turned suddenly from Jekyll to Hyde. 'I might have bloodywell known.'

'Goodbye, love.'

'Get knotted.'

'Language!'

I went my beleaguered way in search of an ordinary workingman's boozer. There wasn't one, it seemed, and when the novelty of being sweet-talked by an endless succession of nubile young playthings began to wear slightly thin, I detoured back to the Reeperbahn. When I reached the end, I crossed the wide dual carriageway to plod back west again. The streets leading south off the Reeperbahn run down to the Altona docks. An area, I thought, which must surely be served by non-tourist hostelries. I walked as far as Davidstrasse, and the huge barn-like fortress of the Davidswache police station which dominates the corner there. Right again, past a line of off-duty prowl cars, to get into Hans-Albert-Platz and there, almost within spitting distance of one of the city's most powerful concentration of the forces of law and order, I found the murkiest action thus far.

I was pestered by blatant, incessant touting, and not just for good clean sex. The little streets surrounding the square were lined with establishments offering every conceivable form of perversion. Some new even to me. The infamous Straight Street in old Valetta, known by generations of randy matelots simply as The Gut, couldn't even begin to compare. I was propositioned by men dressed as women, women dressed as men, and others whose gender I could not determine. The crowds were thickening now. A crocodile of chattering Japanese tourists, enough to fill a bus, was shepherded along the narrow pavements by a trio of bored-looking guides, one male and two big fierce females. I side-stepped into a doorway to avoid being caught up in the throng and so, inadvertently, found my boozer.

That universal odour of beer, and the mindless din of a juke box. An unvarnished L-shaped bar, with plastic-topped stools. The plain wooden tables ranged around two walls were backed by long fitted benches and fronted by bentwood chairs. The tipplers fell into two categories: a polyglot crowd of rough-looking deckhands, and some equally rough-looking whores. A noisome gaggle of shop-worn scrubbers too old for the carriage trade. It must have seemed as though I was slumming. I ordered a glass of beer, then changed my mind and asked for a bottle. Furtive eyes watched me wipe the neck and the barmaid, a stringy little hard-case blonde, asked if I wanted a straw. Behind me, somebody tittered. I took a pull at the ale, which was warm and gassy. Not worth the belly-room. I determined to drink it, though, and not just because of what it would cost.

'Two marks,' the barmaid said.

Two marks was too much, and she knew it. 'I'll give you one-fifty,' I said, 'and just for your nerve, you can keep the change.'

I said it loud and clear, and my shaft of wit raised raucous laughter. 'That's the style, mate!' a Scots voice said. 'Dinnae let the wee bitch screw you – an' I do mean either way!'

I turned. The Scots seaman was slouched on a stool at the other end of the bar. He was pretty far gone, but not too far to have grasped the situation correctly. Probably from my tone. He raised his glass in a wavering salute.

'Here's tae us!'

'Wha's like us?' I said.

'Ye hear that, Alec?' he roared. He lurched about on his teetering stool to aim a drunken nudge at a man who was cursing monotonously into a pay phone fixed to the wall. 'Ne'er mind thon bliddy auld whoor, mon!' he bellowed. 'This felly's ane o' *us*! C'moan, c'moan, let's all ha'e a dram!'

Alec warded off his oppo with one hand while he kept up a steady stream of repetitive vituperation into the telephone. As they pawed and pushed at each other I finished off my beer and put down the bottle and made my exit. I no longer felt the need. I wouldn't have minded a pint of Tetley's, but that stuff was something else. And for what they charged, they could keep it.

I pressed on towards the docks, and soon left the sleazy glitter behind me. The road overlooking the Elbe, lit only by street lamps and almost deserted, was lined with chandlers' stores and junk shops and cheap little eating places. Beneath a couple of hissing pressure lamps placed on the broad harbour wall, a seller of sea-shells plied his late trade, his wares laid out on sacks. Conches and clams

32

and abilone, chambered nautilus, scorpion shells, and various cowries all differing greatly in size and ranging in quality from fair to awful. Most were badly chipped, but here and there a soft-glowing beauty. I slowed as I passed the display, and the vendor closed in hopefully.

'They are all very cheap, sir,' he said.

He looked and moved like an old ex-pug, but for all his shambling size his manner was diffident and curiously gentle. The hesitant, whispering voice was the product of a battered larynx. His nose had been broken, and set, and broken and re-set and broken again. A look at one of his ears and the thickened brows and the dead-white scar tissue which quilted his lips confirmed his erstwhile profession beyond any shadow of doubt. I thought his face looked vaguely familiar, but he'd be too old. Before my time. Perhaps I might remember later.

'What d'you call cheap?' I said. I stooped to pick up an undamaged conch. 'This one, for instance – how much?'

He took it from me and turned it over in his great, knobbly-knuckled hands, and pursed his lips in a soundless whistle. I smelled bad schnapps on his breath. He fondled the shell as though it were fragile.

'Ah, that's a good one,' he said. 'A good one. You've picked the best of the bunch.'

I couldn't honestly argue with him. 'All right, how much then?' I said.

His face puckered up in a worried frown and he nursed the shell to his chest as if reluctant to part with the thing. As though to warm it against his thick jersey.

'How much?' I said again.

'*Zwanzig mark?*'

He was asking, not telling. I could easily have beaten him down, but apart from the fact that I hadn't the heart, the air by the river was cold. Too cold to stand around haggling. Twenty marks – five pounds. By German standards most reasonable. In fact, it was really quite cheap.

'You've got a deal. I'll have it.'

'You are satisfied?' he said.

'If I wasn't, I'd have told you. Here, take your money,' I said.

There was, of course, no question of wrapping, and the shell, which weighed three or four pounds, was too big to go into my raincoat pocket. No matter. I was tired of wandering around, and was thinking now in terms of bed. My bed at the Schloss Hotel. My lonely couch. I felt physically sated. All that touting had put me right off.

So I set out briskly, no longer meandering, towards St Pauli U-bahn station carrying the shell in one hand, wearing it on my fist like a mitten. The interior felt oddly warm, and wonderfully satin-smooth. It was a very handsome thing, and I hoped Mrs Tidy was going to like it. As a present for seeing to the dogs. Because what do you give a proud old lass who *knows* that she already has everything? Not flowers – her house was a potted jungle, and her garden a riot of blooms. Not a brooch, or beads. She scorned such adornments, wore only a wedding band. Not money; she'd be offended. Certainly not chocolates or sweets, for she '. . . wouldn't put such muck in her mouth'. Yes, I thought the conch would do fine, and felt pleased with myself for having bought it.

Too pleased with myself by far, and stupidly lax. Unforgivably careless. I had followed the dockside road, to cut through the empty tree-shaded gardens round the Bismarck Monument. They took me from behind, making no more sound than scurrying mice. I heard the slight scufflings too late, and tried to turn as the first one hit me. He must have been using a cosh and, lucky for me, he was that mite too eager. Instead of finding the skull, he caught me where the neck joins the shoulder. A massive crushing blow which almost put me under and felled me down on my knees.

Dizzy as I was, that hellish Sutherland training triggered off one of the moves so painfully earned from the mad McVicar. I threw mysef forward, fast, and twisted and as my shoulder hit I pivoted on one hip and scythed both legs round just clear of the ground. The backs of my heels struck his shins with a crack and swept him, arms flailing, clean off his feet. He toppled with a yell, straight into the path of one of his buddies. A third man dodged aside and rushed me as I scrambled half-upright. He thought I would rise all the way, but I didn't. I butted him hard in the groin. As he folded over my head, I threw him off my back with a sideways twist. He hooked an arm round my neck, and tried to pull me down with him. My right fist was still wearing the shell like a cumbersome knuckleduster. I swung with all my strength and smashed again at his private parts. He dropped away from me then and crashed to the ground, choking and retching, curled up on his side.

All of this happened in fifteen seconds, then the others were back on their feet. But so, now, was I, and facing them. No sound but that of our laboured breathing and the faint squeak of soft-soled shoes as, this time, they moved in warily. Dim light from a pale quarter-moon merged with the glow from distant street-lamps to filter through the trees and show me what I was up against. The one on my left was big. Not extra tall, but broad and solid, heavy on his feet. Him on my right was the eager beaver, the one who had tackled me first. This time, he wouldn't be so hasty. He moved with a cat-like grace, smacking the cosh on the palm of one hand. He was the dangerous lad. The other was slow, and had only his fists. I didn't think they were pros, because had they been pros I'd have stood no chance. I wouldn't be still on my feet. As they started slowly to crowd me I began to

35

back away, taking care not to stumble over the one I had put on the deck. They made no sudden move, and I dared to hope they hadn't realized I was trying to reach a tree. Get my back against something.

Some hope. The sap-carrier made a fleeting signal and eased around on my flank, making me glance from side to side to keep them both in view. Then the big man worked a flanker as well, and the tactic forced me to choose and I chose the smooth-mover. Or so he thought. My choosing him was a feint, and I turned my sideways lunge towards him into a fast about-face, and I wouldn't have swapped that hard knobbly conch for its weight in solid gold. The big man blundered headlong into a swinging round-arm hook, and I wasn't pulling any punches. There was a loud sick crunching sound as his nose, and maybe his jawbone, was crushed and I knew as he collapsed that he, at least, was out of it. The cosh artist jumped in behind, but his vicious chop at the crown of my head was made to miss its mark by my backwards-slamming elbow. The jolt caught him under the ribs and knocked him off his balance, but the cosh landed high on my cheek at that very tender spot where the bone is least padded. A rush of scalding tears, and my skull exploded with shattering pain. Bright stars blazed in front of my eyes, and as I felt myself reeling I sensed him push me away to give himself room for another swing. Half senseless as I was, I knew in that split second that if he got one in, it was good night Marcus Aurelius. There wasn't time to turn, so I hurled myself backwards against him and the pair of us went down. With me on top. All sixteen stone.

The wind whooshed out of his lungs, and his chops with the sap lost power. As he struggled to slug at me, I twisted half over and caught his wrist and then I knew he was mine. I shifted my weight to pin him down and raised my trusty shell and smashed at his face as he turned his head. He opened his mouth to scream, but the sound never got past his tonsils. It died in the back of his throat, a horrible rasping gargle. I rolled off his crumpled bulk, and rested on my hands and knees to fill my aching lungs with snorting gulps of the cool night air. I shook my throbbing head, scattering big fat droplets of sweat, mustering the strength to rise and move on.

When I finally got to my feet I was mildly startled to find that my triumph had been witnessed. A teenage boy, and a girl. They were standing a dozen yards down the path, rooted to the spot, gaping as though they were petrified. Not a word was said. I could not see their faces distinctly, and I hoped they couldn't see mine. As we stared at each other I suddenly became aware of the sounds of someone else approaching. Voices beyond the trees. The courting couple switched their gaze to the three men on the ground, two of whom were groaning and stirring. Time to be moving on.

Still lugging the shell, I turned away and set off at a brave old trot away from the path and over the grass through a clump of blossoming trees. Once out of sight I doubled back towards the Reeperbahn and ploughed across a flower-bed, puffing and wheezing, and climbed the low stone wall which borders the park along Cuxhaven Allee. Safe over, I slowed to a walk, looking for a taxi. I saw one, and flagged it down, but the driver took one look at me and accelerated sharply away. I cursed his dwindling tail-lights.

'*Was ist los, leibchen?*'

The question came from behind and above. I turned round and looked up, taking care to stay in deep shadow. She was leaning out of a first-floor window, halo-ed by dim pink light. The window-sill had a cushion on it.

'*Was ist los?*' she asked again.

'Nothing.' Warm stuff ran down my neck.

'Are you looking for a girl?'

She hadn't been a girl for thirty years, but: 'I might be, at that,' I said.

'Come on up then, sweetheart. The front door is open.'

A small apartment block, very probably purpose-built. The hall and stairs were laid with good carpet, everything ruthlessly clean, and the air made fragrant with aerosol spray. As I started stiffly to climb, a door opened up on the landing above. She was definitely past her prime, but she bulged in all the right places and her face wore a welcoming smile. When the light from her open door fell on me, the welcome faded fast. She gasped and stepped back quickly and made to close the door. I let her see a fistful of big ones.

'Please, Fräulein – wait!' I said. 'I've been mugged, but they did not get my money . . .' She looked at the bundle of notes, then back at my face, and hesitated. 'Please . . .' I said again.

'You're a foreigner, aren't you?'

'American.'

'Yes, I thought so,' she said. 'Listen, I don't want trouble.'

'My God, of course not!' I said.

She made up her mind. 'Come in, then.'

She stood away from the door to let me precede her into the room. A heavy, scented fug composed in parts of perfumes and face-paint, the musky secretions of sex, and deodorized perspiration. That curious love-nest smell. The little white poodle curled up on a mat in front of the square tiled stove raised its head to quiz me with shiny black eyes. Its mistress closed the door, and turned to me, and held out a hand. Pink palm upwards, of course, so not for shaking. For taking.

'Money first, darling,' she said.

She looked like your pro of legend and fable, the one with a heart of gold. But her made-up eyes were bright as the poodle's, and her generous open smile was slightly less real than plastic flowers. The fair, wavy locks were her own, as was the albeit-overweight figure. The filmy négligee only served to enhance her swelling curves, and did nothing at all to hide large brown aureoles with thimble-like nipples. A thick brush of pubic hair. Though her legs were still good, her upper arms were just beginning to sag. So too was her second chin. But there was plenty of mileage left in her, and taken in the round, she was still an attractive old trouper. She preened coyly under my stare, and popped the standard question.

'You like it, sweetheart?' she said.

'Yes, not half!' I said. 'Do you do all night or just short time?'

'Oh, short time, darling,' she said. 'Unless you want to spend four hundred marks . . .'

'No, I bloodywell don't!' I said. I said it in English.

'*Bitte?*'

'I've only got half an hour to spare.'

She chuckled. 'It won't take *that* long, sweetheart.'

'Do you mind if I clean up first?'

She frowned. 'Time is money, darling.'

'All right, how much?' I said.

She eyed me shrewdly. Who was I fooling. 'You do not wish to make love.' Not a query. A bold, flat statement.

'I want to get cleaned up,' I said.

'There are public toilets along at St Pauli.'

Public was the word. 'Listen,' I said, 'what about it?'

'Give me one hundred,' she said.

'Christ,' I said, 'that's fifty dollars.' Or just over £25.

She shrugged. 'I told you – time is money.'

I counted out the notes. Her little fist closed over them and she pointed at a door. 'That is the bathroom. Leave me your coat.'

I laid the shell on a lace-covered table and eased off my dust-covered coat and looked at myself in the bathroom mirror. Had I been a woman living alone, I wouldn't have let me in. My face was a battered, gory mess. I even had blood in my hair. The cheek split open by the cosh had already begun to swell, pushing up the bottom eyelid. The top of my forehead was bruised, a result, no doubt, of my butting. I filled the blue basin with clean cold water and started to swab away with a flannel I found on the end of the bath. The wound high up on my cheek looked as though it might need stitches. When I had dabbed it clean, it started at once to bleed again. I needed a pad of lint and a strip of sticking plaster.

'Fräulein . . .'

'*Bitte?*'

She appeared at the open door, my coat in one hand, a brush in the other.

'Do you have a dressing, please?'

She looked at my face, and nodded. 'Just a moment,' she said. 'When I've finished your raincoat, I'll see to that for you.'

She proved as good as her word. She made me perch on the edge of the bath and stood between my knees and got to work with cotton wool and a bottle of iodine. The pungent iodine stung like hell, but she did a very neat job and when she had smoothed on a sticking plaster I made as though to rise.

'No,' she said, 'wait a minute.'

She left me sitting there, and was back directly with a compact of make-up. The flesh-coloured pancake kind. When she was done, I consulted the mirror. Even in that strong light my face looked fairly presentable and after I'd combed my hair I was all set up to hit the road.

'Shall I phone for a taxi?' she said. She noticed my hesitation. That girl was on the ball. She smiled. 'Don't worry, the driver's a good friend of mine. Just give him a decent tip, and he'll forget he ever saw you – and by the way, neither have I.'

I believed her. She was earning her money. As she used the telephone, I put on my freshly brushed raincoat. When the taxi came, she stood on tiptoe to kiss me.

'Perhaps another time?'

'No perhaps about it,' I lied. 'Thanks for everything.'

I rode the taxi right to the Schloss. No point in messing around. The job was obviously blown wide open and the burning question now was how, and by whom, and who were the yobbos? As the porter was getting my key, I thought about ringing Mackenzie's room. But on second thoughts, what the hell. Let him get a good night's sleep. Stay on top of his form. The way things were moving, he'd damn well better. I needed a strong right arm.

I did a routine check on the room, but nothing had been disturbed. Stiff and sore, I shucked off my clothes and rolled straight into bed. To hell with the callisthenics. I didn't even clean my teeth. When I stretched out an arm to switch off the light I had to reach over the shell, which I'd dumped on the bedside table. I looked at it under the light. Sadly, it was no longer perfect. Useless now as a gift. It was scuffed and chipped and covered in scratch marks, and frayed around the edges.

Like me.

Friday

'What's wrong with the porridge, Mackenzie?'

'I'm afraid I don't like it,' he said.

'Next time, try using sugar.'

'I was brought up to take it with salt.'

'Some sugar for your scrambled eggs?'

'No thanks, but after you with the pepper,' he said. He grinned as he watched me at work with the grinder, ' – that's if there'll be any left.'

Whatever else the lad was short of, it certainly wasn't restraint. He had not mentioned my battle scars, or asked what I'd done to my face. We finished the rest of our breakfast in silence, as civilized people should. When I had poured my fourth cup of tea, and he had declined a third, I looked at him across the table.

'Well, come on then,' I said. 'Get it over with. Ask me.'

'Ask you what, sir?' he said.

'Don't call me sir. Where I got the shiner.'

'I wouldn't presume to!' he said. He appeared to be mildly affronted. I told him, anway, and he listened without interrupting. Then: 'With respect,' he went on, 'I think we ought to have stuck together.'

'You know something, Jock?' I said, 'you could be right.'

'Who were they?'

'I haven't a clue,' I said. 'I couldn't stick around to find out. Not without attracting a crowd, and we don't need that sort of publicity.'

'Good heavens, of course not,' he said.

'I assume you realize this means we're blown here?'

'Well . . . they could have been after your cash.'

'They could have been, yes, but they weren't.'

'But how could anyone possibly know?'

'Ask me another,' I said. 'But somebody knows, and that's a fact.'

'I can't understand it,' he said.

'Don't try. It'll all come out in the wash.'

'So what are we going to do now?'

'We're going up to Lübeck, aren't we – and keep your voice down,' I said.

The waiter was settling an elderly couple at the table next to ours, which was well within eavesdropping distance. The old dears looked harmless enough, but so did Baby Face Nelson.

'Listen, you finished?' I said. 'Right, let's go up to my room.'

I had packed my gear before going down to breakfast, and my suitcase lay on the bed. Mackenzie nodded at it.

'Are you leaving, too?' he said, 'I thought you were meant to be staying on here?'

'What – after last night?' I said. 'We're getting lost Jock, you and me both.'

'Where do we lose ourselves?'

'In Lübeck-Travemunde.'

'But if we're blown down here – '

'You'd better hope it's *only* down here. If the Lübeck bit's been blown, we might as well bugger off back to Blighty.'

'But surely if the Others know . . .'

'I didn't say the Others knew, I just said the job was blown. We're not the only ones after Jagersberg – or so old Harvester says.'

'You never told me he told you that.'

'There was no need for you to know. Now there is.'

'I see,' he said. 'What I don't see, though, is what makes you so sure it wasn't the Others who put the boot in last night.'

'Simple, lad,' I said, 'the Others wouldn't have ponced around trying to rough me up, they'd have taken me out. I'd be dead now.'

'Unless, of course, it was meant as a warning – '

'Warning, my arse!' I said. 'They'd have killed me. You, too. Remember that.'

'I suppose you're right.'

'Don't just suppose. *Remember.* This isn't a training run. This is where they use real bullets.'

'And what do we use?' he said.

'Low cunning.'

'I see.'

'No, you don't see. I haven't told you yet. Listen carefully, Mackenzie, here's what we're going to do . . .'

We checked out and left the hotel together, just after a quarter to nine, and taxi-ed up to the Hauptbahnhof. Mackenzie watched the bags, while I used one of the public phones in the teeming concourse there. Harvester was an early bird, and the number he had given me must have been that of a direct line to his office. He answered at the third ring.

'Harvester, Trade and Technology.'

'This line sterile?' I said.

'Oh, it's you, Farrow – yes, it's quite clean.'

'Listen, then,' I said, 'I want a safe car for a couple of days.'

'A car? What for?' he said.

'I said a *safe* car.'

'I heard you. When do you want it?'

'As of right now,' I said. 'How soon can you deliver?'

'Deliver where?' he said.

Rahlstedt S-bahn station.'

'That's fifteen miles from here!'

'I know how far it is – how soon?'

A pause. 'Eleven o'clock okay?'

'I'd rather it was half past ten.'

'What's all the rush?' he said. 'Complications?'

'You've hit it.'

'Right. Ten-thirty,' he said.

The line went dead as he broke the connection. So the stories about him were true, and he really was unflappable. I hoped so, anyway. I rejoined Mackenzie, waiting by the bags.

'Spot anything?' I said.

He shook his head. 'I don't think so, but it's difficult to say.'

It was, of course. Hamburg's splendid main railway station is a very busy place at any time of the day or night. Now, in the midst of the morning rush hour, S-bahn and U-bahn commuters mingled with main-line passengers in a jostling, seething throng. The crowds were both a help and a hindrance.

'All right, let's go,' I said.

We picked up our traps and took to the steps leading down on to platform thirteen just as a swaying train rumbled in. Its indicator said POPPENBÜTTEL. Mackenzie boarded the train, and leaped off again just as the doors were closing. Nobody followed suit, and both of us caught the next train in. We travelled to Hasselbrook and, when we alighted, split up as planned. Mackenzie followed the signs which pointed the way to the interchange tunnel leading to the S4 Ahrensburg line. Five other people made the switch with him. I took careful note of them all from a vantage point by the refreshment kiosk. I ordered a cup of tea, and drank it slowly. It tasted foul. Ten or twelve minutes later, another train rumbled in. Before it could discharge its passengers I hurried off on the route taken by Mackenzie. He was waiting for me on the near-deserted platform.

'Train gone, has it?' I said.

'Yes. I counted five transfers.'

'We might well be clean, then,' I said.

'Do we still work the double at Rahlstedt?'

'Damn right we work it,' I said. 'Just observe the original briefing.'

'What about tickets?' he said.

'Bugger the tickets. We'll risk it.'

The German railways operate a system which our unions would never permit, for the simple reason it's much too efficient. The traveller obtains his fixed-price ticket from one of numerous slot-machines, and is never hindered by gate-checks to make sure he's got the thing. Bottlenecks at stations are thus averted, but inspectors who roam certain trains are empowered to levy on-the-spot fines of twenty times the fare. It is possible to travel on the network for days and weeks on end without once being asked for one's ticket, but such is the inherent native discipline, offenders are virtually unknown.

During the long northbound ride to Rahlstedt the crowd in our carriage thinned out until, as we approached the station, only two others remained. A couple of chattering teenage girls. I was tempted to change the plan and get off there with Mackenzie, straight into the waiting car, and away at once to Lübeck. But having already snapped at Mackenzie for suggesting we do just that, I could hardly falter now. As the train slowed, I nodded at him.

'Off you go, then,' I said.

He nipped off smartly, carrying both of our bags. The teenage girls stayed on and rode with me to the terminus, five miles up the line. I tailed them out of the clean little station and watched them saunter away towards the looming towers of the castle. Low, scudding clouds loosed a spatter of rain. I turned up the collar of my Burberry and set out after the girls, along the broad sidewalk of Hamburgstrasse. They crossed at the first set of lights. I stayed where I was on the right-hand side, heading north with the traffic flow. I walked on the outer edge of the pavement, straight on through the smart little town, until Hamburgstrasse became Lübeckstrasse. The faltering shower of rain burgeoned into a steady downpour. Where the *hell* was the car.

It pulled up close alongside me and Mackenzie leaned across to release the door and push it open. I scrambled in, out of the rain, and he let out the clutch as I slammed the door shut.

'Christ, lad, what kept you?' I said.

'Traffic. Trains are much faster than cars.'

'Any trouble?'

'None,' he said. He stayed in third gear and rammed his foot down to overtake a truck, then slid into top, and settled back. 'I certainly wasn't tailed when I got off the train at Rahlstedt.'

'Yes, well, it's quite likely,' I said, 'that we haven't been tailed at all today, but there's nothing like making sure – look, slow down, for God's sake! We're not on the autobahn yet!'

He grinned. 'It's all right, I'm an Advanced Driver.'

'I don't give a monkeys,' I said. 'And I *don't* want a ticket for speeding.'

Lübeck lies north-east of Hamburg at a distance of forty miles, with Ahrensburg roughly halfway between them, just off the main motorway. Once we had picked up the autobahn, I gave Mackenzie the nod to go ahead and test the car's potential. It was one of the big German Fords, their version of the Granada. Quite a useful machine, and obviously in first-class condition. We easily topped the ton, and Mackenzie said the car handled well – for a mass-production job.

'I suppose you're used to Rolls-Royces, Jock.'

'No, not really,' he said. 'Actually, I drive a Jensen.'

'Very nice,' I said. 'Just don't forget you're not driving it now.'

'Where do I head for?' he said.

'We'll have a quick shufti at Lübeck first – we must be nearly there – and then we'll go on to Travemunde.'

'Will you stay at the Maritim?'

'Just depends. I'll decide when we've seen this bloke Fischer. Look, switch your wipers off, they're getting on my bloody nerves.'

We had left the rain behind, and were running into a rising wind. Gusts of it rocked the car, and tore at the tarpaulin load-covers of the snarling juggernauts which jostled for position along the two nearside lanes. In a little under fifteen minutes we had raised the Lübeck sign, and Mackenzie slowed down for the turn-off. We did the clover-leaf bit and dropped down on to Fackenburger Allee and as we rolled into town, with the Hauptbahnof over to our right, I began to recognize landmarks. It all came back to me.

Lübeck, once a Hanseatic republican state, is an ancient and very beautiful city. The original medieval settlement, now known as the Old Town, is built on an island a little more than a mile in width and half again as long, formed by the rivers Trave and Wakenitz. This natural fortress is surrounded on all sides by a sprawl of largely self-contained suburbs of which Travemunde, nine miles north, is easily the most widely known. Blankensee, five miles south, is where the wartime airfield was situated and where, in that terrible winter of 1945, I spent the coldest six months of my life.

As we negotiated the big traffic roundabout at the end of the Holstentor Platz, I spotted a newsagent's shop on the corner.

'Pull up over there, Jock,' I said.

I paid five marks for a *stadtplan* with Lübeck on one side and Travemunde on the other, only to find, when I got back into the car, that Mackenzie was struggling to unfold an identical item.

'Where the hell did you get that, Mackenzie?'

'Glove compartment,' he said.

'You might have bloodywell told me before I blew twenty-five bob!'

'I didn't know it was in there.'

'Oh well, never mind. Listen, we've got about a couple of hours. I think we'll leave the car here. I'm not sure there's parking space over in the Old Town.'

We locked up all round and set off on foot to cross the river by the way of the Holstentorbrücke, passing through the narrow arched gateway which seems to keep the pair of massive round brick towers, with their conical slate roofs, from falling inwards upon each other. It was still somewhat windy, but mercifully dry.

'Do you want us to separate?' Mackenzie asked.

'Yes, but let's have a coffee first.'

We chose a little café on the edge of the old market-place, facing the vaulted stone cloisters of the thirteenth-century town hall. I unfolded my map on the red check tablecloth, and Mackenzie drew round his chair. The island town is traversed lengthways by two long thorough-fares which run roughly parallel and are crossed by a network of lesser streets, some of them very narrow, falling east and west off the long low hogback to the water on either side. Königstrasse, Lübeck's main street, stretches from the ages-old Burgtor gate at the northern tip of the island to the Mühlenbrücke in the south. A waiter brought our coffees and we sipped them, studying form.

'Not much danger of getting lost here,' said Mackenzie.

'Don't get too cocky,' I said. 'Just make sure you take it all in.'

'Do you want us to do it like last time – me tail you, I mean?'

'That's right. Come on, we'd better get started.'

First thing I did, I called at an optician's on Königstrasse and bought a pair of sunglasses to hide my swollen eye. The cut had scabbed over during the night, and would not need a stitch after all, but that side of my face felt stiff and painful. When I left the shop I turned south towards the Mühlenbrücke, walking slowly and fixing landmarks firmly in mind. I actually enjoyed the ninety-minute stroll and was glad, as I wandered around, to see that no evidence remained of the devastating incendiary attack launched by RAF bombers during the Easter of '42. The splendid old buildings, many of them dating from the eleventh and twelfth centuries, had been lovingly restored, and I saw too that the depredations of post-war property boys had been confined to the outer suburbs. I paced my tour of the Old Town carefully, so that at a quarter to one I was back at the Holstentor gate, just a very short way from the car. There was a parking ticket taped to the windscreen. I tore it off and threw it into the litter basket clamped to a nearby bus-stop shelter. Then I got into the passenger seat to wait for my shadow. He tapped on the window a few minutes later, and I opened the door for him.

'Well?' I asked him.

'Nothing,' he said, 'you were clean every step of the way.'

'You sure?'

'Yes, I'm certain.'

'Good. Let's go, then.'

He drove us up to Travemunde in fifteen minutes flat, and we parked in the underground garage of the Hotel Maritim. I had already decided to check in at the Maritim, using my Herbert Stroud cover. We were shown to our separate rooms, and after a quick wash to freshen up,

50

I joined Mackenzie down in the restaurant. As the lunch progressed, I was moved to wonder why no Willi Fischer. When he still hadn't made an appearance as I re-filled my coffee cup, I began to wonder in earnest. Then I spotted a porter moving between the tables to display a paging board with 'Herr Stroud Please' chalked across it. I stood up to beckon the man, and he made his way across to us.

'Herr Stroud?' I nodded. 'There is a telephone call for you, sir. You can take it in any of the booths in the lobby.'

'Very well, thank you,' I said. I nodded then at Mackenzie. 'All right, you know the drill.'

He watched my back as I took the call. I closed myself in the booth, and lifted the receiver. He had a hoarse, almost sibilant voice.

'Is that Herr Stroud speaking?'

'Yes, it is,' I said.

'The *Inga*, a four-metre cabin cruiser, moored along the strand.'

'Well,' I said, 'what about it?'

'I'll be there in fifteen minutes.'

'Will you now?' I said. 'And who might you be?'

'Fischer.'

'All right, see you,' I said.

Mackenzie was browsing at the magazine stand over on the other side of the lobby. He joined me at the door, we went out into the windy sunshine. We walked through the complex of shops between the hotel and the sea, and set out along the esplanade towards the forest of masts by the strand. Mackenzie quizzed me.

'Fischer?'

'That's what he told me,' I said.

'You still worried?'

'I'm always worried. That's how I've lived so long.'

That walk along the front was a real revelation. The coast at Travemunde is shaped like a blunt arrow-head, the north face of which is exposed to the Baltic. That part of the wedge to the south looks out across a narrow channel less than half a mile wide. The eastern bank of the sheltered creek is formed by a narrow-necked isthmus shaped like a vulture's beak, most of it part of Travemunde. The border cuts across the neck of the isthmus to create a sort of Western outpost. All the rest is Deutsche Demokratische Republik. Travemunde is a holiday resort which caters for people with plenty of money, and the moorings along the strand were jam-packed with big sleek yachts. In spite of its being so early in the season there was plenty going on, and it was easily seen that in the season the place would hum like a hive.

But in grim stark contrast, the glorious stretch of soft white sand beyond the border on the eastern side was absolutely deserted. Not so much as a dog. Just above the high-water mark a line of forbidding watchtowers, perhaps a couple of hundred yards apart, stretched as far as the eye could see. Droning and whickering loud over-head, an East German helicopter circled endlessly, maintaining a constant daytime surveillance.

Mackenzie whistled softly. 'Looks a bit daunting,' he said.

'Christ, don't bang on about it. I'm daunted enough as it is.'

We picked out the *Inga* quite easily, because not only was she one of the smallest craft on the moorings, her hull was painted dark green. All the better for night work, of course, but among that gathering of clean white shapes she was sticking out a mile. Still, you can't have it both ways, as Charlie would doubtless have said. She was tied up stern-on to a floating pontoon, underneath the wall, bobbing gently on the swell. There were curtains across her side-screens, and no sign of life on board.

'Do you want me to come with you?'

'No, you hang about, Jock,' I said.

He waited up on the jetty, to watch me step across her

transom and knock on the cabin hatch. It was opened almost instantly.

'Herr Stroud?'

'That's me,' I said.

'I am Fischer. Please come in.'

'Just a minute,' I said. I turned and beckoned Mackenzie.

'Who is that man?' Fischer said.

A friend. Have you any objections?'

'No, of course not,' he said.

He backed down off the three-step companionway and I ducked in after him. The cabin was small, and the deckhead was low. I had to bend my head. There was the usual drop-leaf table bolted to the deck, flanked by bunks which served as seats. A hatch in the tiny for'ard bulkhead probably opened on to the loo. Fischer moved to a locker on the port side aft, and turned with his hand on the latch.

'Would you care for a drink?'

'No, thanks,' I said, 'I've just had my lunch – come in, Jock, and shut the door.' I looked back at Fischer, and pointed up for'ard. 'That the toilet in there?' He nodded. 'Mind if I use it?'

His wide and rather fleshy lips twisted in a grin. He knew what I was up to. 'Please – help yourself,' he said.

There was no one hidden in the minute compartment. Hell, what did I expect? I didn't even bother to go through the motions. I just stepped out again. Fischer still wore his little grin.

'Are you satisfied now, Herr Stroud?'

I moved across to the starboard side and sat by Mackenzie. 'I'll answer that,' I said, 'after we've had a natter.'

'Then by all means let us begin.'

There was a large rolled-up chart on the table, Fischer spread it out and weighted the corners with odds and ends taken from the pockets of his reefer jacket, a little compass, a heavy brass cigarette lighter, and a penknife with silver mounts. He held down the other corner with one of his strong brown hands. As he busied himself, I studied the man. Something about him vaguely disturbed me, though I could not think what it was. His short black hair was thick and curly, just starting to show some grey, and his swarthy features were heavily lined. Dark eyes under beetling brows were set each side of a nose which hooked away to flaring nostrils. A short upper lip, and a resolute chin deeply cleft in its centre. Hardly an Aryan face, although German was obviously his native tongue. He looked about forty years old. Not a very tall man, but he emanated power. His shoulders were broad and his chest was deep.

'The old Ost Strand,' he said. A grease-rimmed finger-nail scratched at the chart, tracing the beach with its string of watchtowers. 'This is where we will pick up Herr Jagersberg.'

'Is that a fact?' I said. 'I bet that coast's just lousy with mines.'

'Oh, yes. The sea, too,' he said. 'There are also many sensors.'

'Heat, light, sound, and movement?'

'All of those,' he said, 'and perhaps some we don't even know about yet. What we do know is that some of them can tell the difference between a herring and a kipper.'

'They're both the same fish,' Mackenzie said.

'They can *still* tell the difference.'

I believed him. 'That's marvellous,' I said, 'so how the hell do we take a boat in?'

'We do not take a boat in,' he said. 'The boat will be moored here' – he stabbed at the map – 'in the lee of the channel buoy.'

I checked the scale of the map, and began to calculate distances. From the broad blunt nose of the arrowhead coastline there swept out into the sea the long curving arm of a massive breakwater with a squat lighthouse perched on the end. The big red buoy was anchored out in the channel entrance some three hundred yards away, at a point exactly midway between the lighthouse and the seaward end of a heavy steel-mesh boom floated out to mark the border. The line of cylindrical floats looked to be about three hundred yards long, too. A total of nine hundred yards, then, from the lighthouse to the spot where the boom met the shore. The forty-storey Maritim Hotel, clearly marked on the map, stood fewer than a hundred yards back from the tip of the arrowhead. So, from the Maritim roof to the eastern shoreline, say a thousand yards. I looked up, and my eyes met Fischer's.

'Right, tell us how it's done.'

He fumbled in the pockets of his dark blue jacket for a pack of cigarettes, lit one, and coughed up a cloud of wet smoke.

'Yes, of course,' he said. His forefinger moved across the map and stopped at a cluster of neat black rectangles a mile or so inland. Four roads radiating away from the rectangles ran to equidistant spots on the beach, and a fifth dead-straight road ran down to the border across the isthmus neck. 'The Voppo barracks are here, and here' – he indicated a sizable town about twenty-five miles farther east, 'is the power station at Wismar. We have people working there.'

'I take it you mean they can shut off the juice, but you're not going to tell me,' I said, 'that the barracks doesn't have its own generator?'

'Oh, naturally,' he said, 'but it is used in emergencies only.' Again that sardonic grin. 'No matter, we have friends in the barracks also.'

'But the sensors are surely self-powered,' said Mackenzie.

'That is correct,' Fischer said, 'but with no power to the receiving and monitoring equipment . . .'

'Quite. But it's too dicey,' I said. 'Suppose your chums don't deliver this breakdown?'

'They *will* deliver it,' he said.

'The Voppos will still know there's something going on.'

He shrugged. 'That is true,' he said, 'but they will not know what, and they will not know where.'

'Give over, Fischer,' I said. 'It's going to be perfectly obvious.'

'Please hear me out,' he said. 'Other friends have arranged for certain diversions, and – '

'Jesus Christ!' I said, 'just how many blokes are in on this thing?'

'All they know,' Fischer said, 'is that we, over here, have a list of requirements.'

'Well, I don't like it,' I said.

'You are playing the devil's advocate.'

'Damned right I am,' I said. 'It's my bloody neck on the block – remember?'

'It is not only yours, Herr Stroud. A lot of others are taking grave risks.'

'That's no great comfort to *me*.'

'Do you wish to hear the rest of it, then?'

'We might as well,' I said. 'I just hope it gets a bit better, that's all.'

Fischer stubbed out his foul cigarette, and immediately lit another. The little boat rocked on the swell of something substantial steaming up-channel. Mackenzie cleared his throat.

'Something bothering you, is there, Jock?'

'I was thinking of mines,' he said.

'Yes,' Fischer said, 'I was coming to that. The mines are no problem at all. We have managed to obtain a detector.'

'Will it work under water, as well?'

'No, but the need does not arise. There are no mines close to the boom, because the currents might wash them against it and blow the whole thing sky-high. So, if you swim hard alongside it – '

'Just a minute,' I said, 'did you say *swim*? Why *not* use the boat?'

'The boat must stay by the buoy. It would present too big a target, even in the dark. But the Voppos will not fire on her so long as she's west of the buoy.'

'So we're supposed to swim six hundred yards. How old is Jagersberg?'

'I believe he is nearly seventy.'

'Christ Almighty!' I said.

'You will wear inflatable jackets, Herr Stroud.'

'Even so,' I said, 'it's very damned cold in the Baltic, and cold saps the strength, you know. Especially that of a seventy-year-old. Does *he* know what's to be done?'

'Yes, and he says he can do it.'

'Then I wish I had his faith.'

Fischer sighed, and shook his head. 'Believe me, Herr Stroud,' he said, 'it can be done.'

'Maybe it can,' I said, 'but this way? Man, there are too many factors – and it needs just one to go wrong.'

'We have planned it very carefully.'

'Oh, I'm sure you have,' I said. 'Gallipoli was planned very carefully.'

'*Bitte?*'

'Never mind. All right, let's hear the rest of it. Take it step by step.'

When Fischer leaned back against the bulkhead, one corner of the map curled up. He let it. We did not need the map now. He lit yet another cigarette. No wonder his larynx was cracking up. His voice sounded very hoarse, and from time to time he rubbed his throat.

'. . . and Pablo will take you up to Schonberg – '

I felt a twinge of unease. Fischer knew more than was good for him. Or, rather, more that was good for *me*.

'Hang on,' I broke in, 'who's this Pablo character?'

Fischer looked surprised. 'Why, Pablo is Pablo.'

'Yes, that figures,' I said, 'but who *is* he? Do you know him?'

'I have worked with him twice before.'

'That doesn't answer my question.'

'I know him only by name. But you, of course, will meet him when you go to East Berlin.'

My twinge of unease became a stab. 'Yes, go on,' I said, 'we'd got as far as Schonberg.'

'A pretty little place. Herr Jagersberg has a cottage there. He goes up most weekends.'

'How far is Schonberg from the beach?'

'Fourteen kilometres.'

About ten miles. 'I see,' I said.

'Pablo will take you to Jagersberg's house, then escort you both to the beach.'

I loosed a sarcasm. 'Just like that.'

Fischer shrugged again. 'I do not know the details.'

'I hope to Christ somebody does!'

'Pablo will take good care of you. Anyway,' he went on, 'you will enter the water at 0020.'

'Is that when the power cut starts?'

'Yes, you should keep an eye on the lights in the towers. The moment they go out, the sensors will be rendered useless.'

'How long will the failure last?'

'At most, half an hour. Twenty minutes, at least.'

'You must be kidding!' I said. 'Six hundred yards in twenty minutes? What the hell do you think we are? I'll probably have to tow the old man!'

'The current will help you,' he said. 'This whole operation has been timed to take advantage of the tides.'

'Well, I suppose that's something,' I said. 'But, Jesus,

only twenty minutes. We might just clear the end of the boom.'

'You underestimate yourself, Herr Stroud.'

'Better to do that,' I said, 'than end up a bloody floater.'

'Er . . . hhrmm . . .' Mackenzie said.

'All right, Jock, what is it?'

'Why don't I swim out and give you a hand?'

'I'll tell you why, my old sunshine,' I said, 'you're going to be elsewhere.'

'Oh, I see,' he said.

'Not yet, you don't, but you will in a minute.'

'So I think that is all,' Fischer said.

'No, it isn't. I want a rifle, a high-powered magnum job. Something with one of the latest night-sights.'

'That will not be easy,' he said.

'I didn't ask for it to be easy. Can you get one or not?'

'Exactly what do you have in mind?'

'I couldn't care less what it is, just so long as it has a flat trajectory over a thousand yards, from a height of maybe eighty metres.'

'I might be able to borrow a Husqvarna . . .'

'Jock?'

'That should do,' he said. 'Provided, of course, it's the .270 Special.'

'How soon can you get it?' I said.

'Are you thinking of using it tomorrow night?'

'Right first time,' I said. 'So what about it – yes or no?'

He frowned. 'All right,' he said, 'but if you are making a change of plan – '

'No change of *your* plan,' I said. 'Just don't worry about it.'

'Suppose I cannot get the Husqvarna?'

'If you can't, you can't,' I said. 'We'll have to get one from somewhere else.'

'Leave it with me,' Fischer said. 'Now, do you have any questions?'

'Yes,' Mackenzie said, 'what's the drill if something goes wrong?'

'I'll tell you, Jock,' I said, 'you'll have to find your own way home.'

'You will do it, then?' Fischer said.

'I'll let you know when I've thought it over. But tell me, Fischer,' I said, 'what happens to Jagersberg afterwards?'

'I take him home with me, and dry him off and put him to bed. You pick him up in the morning.'

'It would help if we knew from where.'

'I live at Hundestrasse, 40.'

'Hundestrasse?' I said. 'Isn't that up near the railway station?'

'No, it's in the Old Town,' he said. It was. 'It runs east off Königstrasse. Do you know Lëbeck well?'

'Only from the street plan.'

'That is a pity,' he said. 'Lübeck is a beautiful town.'

'Well, we can't waste time chatting,' I said. 'How soon will you know about the rifle?'

'Perhaps tonight,' he said. 'I will telephone you at the Maritim.'

'No, don't do that,' I said. 'We'll meet you back here – what time can you make it?'

'Shall we say half past ten?'

'Make it eleven.'

'Eleven it is, then.' He held out a sinewy hand, and flashed his big teeth as I shook it. 'I know we are going to succeed.'

I rose and bumped my skull on the deckhead, rocking the little boat, and Mackenzie stood up and rocked it some more. The cabin was full of smoke from Fischer's strong-smelling cigarettes, and I was glad to get out into clean fresh air. When I stepped over the transom after

Mackenzie, our combined weights set the pontoon awash and a playful ripple of chill Baltic water lapped over the tops of my shoes. I gasped and cursed, and Mackenzie looked back.

'Oh, hard lines!' he said.

'Never mind "hard lines", you silly bugger – get *off* the bloody thing!'

He leaped up on to the jetty steps. 'I'm awfully sorry,' he said. 'Come on, I'll buy you a Glenmorangie.'

'Yes – and you'll make it a big one!' I said.

Getting up on to the roof was easy. We just rode the lift to the thirty-eighth floor, transferred to the service stairs, and I let Mackenzie do the lock on the heavy door at the top. He had it open in decent time.

'You've got a nice touch, lad,' I said. 'You're nearly as good as Charlie McGowan.'

'That'll be the day.'

'Yes, well, come on, and keep your head down.'

It was just after half past seven in the evening, and the onset of dusk had brought with it a drop in the wind. A bank of low cloud hung over the Baltic, threatening imminent rain. We stepped out on to the big flat roof with its rows of slatted ventilators and two huge water tanks, and made our way to the parapet which faced the old Ost Strand. Mole and lighthouse and rolling buoy appeared as Dinky toys, and across the channel the line of watchtowers looked almost harmless. From that height, the channel seemed calm.

'I can see now why you want a rifle.'

'I thought you might,' I said. 'Just how good *are* you, Mackenzie?'

'Actually, I'm pretty fair.'

'Never mind the shrinking violet bit – when were you last on the range?'

'Last February.'

61

'Up in *Sutherland*?'

'Yes.'

'Jesus, lad,' I said, 'I hope you've still got all your courting equipment. What was your average then?'

'At the one-thousand-yard mark, ninety-three.'

'Well, I'm damned!' I said. 'Thank God for that small mercy. Things are looking up. Ever shot at a real live person?'

'Er ... no, I haven't.'

'Now's your big chance, then,' I said. 'I want some cover tomorrow night. If the Voppos start throwing shit at us, you're going to throw some back. Make 'em keep their bloody heads down. Think you can do it from here?'

We stared across at the watchtowers. God, they looked miles away.

'I'll do my best, sir.'

I let the 'sir' pass. 'That's good enough for me. Get yourself up here at midnight – okay?'

'Magnum loads make quite a bang. Shouldn't we have asked for a silencer?'

'No, we shouldn't,' I said, 'it would play fun and games with the muzzle velocity.'

'Yes, that's true,' he said.

'And it's more than likely the sound will disperse every which way,' I said. 'It'll be difficult to tell where it's coming from, and by the time some bright spark twigs, the fireworks should be over. Also, don't forget that with luck there'll be no need to shoot. I'm hoping so, anyway.'

'What do I do once I've seen that you're clear?'

'You'd better come down to the boat. Bring the shooter with you.'

'Anything else I can do?'

'I might think of something. Let's go get some dinner. I could eat an underdone horse.'

It looked like a large executive briefcase, slightly longer

than most and perhaps an inch or so deeper. Fischer snapped the heavy brass catches and opened the case so that the two halves lay flat on the cabin table. The Swedish firm of Husqvarna might not make the Rolls-Royce of sniper weapons, but they package their products well. The component parts of the rifle snuggled in padded slots, satiny stock, and breech, and barrel. I picked out the bulky 'scope.

'This isn't a light-intensifying job.'

'I'm sorry,' Fischer said, 'but it *is* infra-red, and it's the best I could get.'

'That be all right for you, Jock?'

Mackenzie was busy assembling the rifle. He did it with practised ease and the parts seemed to marry themselves together, smooth as a Longines watch. He laid the weapon down on the table, and lifted the sight off my hand.

'Mmm . . . the range is a bit much,' he said, 'but yes, I think it might do the job.'

'I don't want you thinking, I want you knowing. Will it or won't it?' I said.

'The answer's yes, then. What about ammo?'

'I have it here,' Fischer said. He fished in the pocket of his reefer jacket and came up with a heavy waxed-cardboard box. 'There are twenty-five rounds – will that be enough?'

'It had better be,' I said, 'because if we need more it'll mean there's big trouble. In which case, we shan't have a prayer.'

'Do I take it, then, that we're going ahead?'

'No, you don't,' I said, 'not until I've talked with this bloke Pablo. Which brings me to something else – how do you two communicate?'

'We never do,' Fischer said. 'All contact is made through Herr Harvester.'

'Yes, I should hope so,' I said, 'but how easy is it to get in touch? I mean, how long does it take?'

'If we are all on alert, half an hour for message and reply.'

'Not bad,' I said. 'Now listen: stand by tomorrow night – '

'But of course!'

' – and I'll pass you the word when I've talked to Pablo.'

'Is there something still troubling you, then?'

'Yes, I don't much care for the beach bit. If it's seeded with the new high-density plastic mines, your metal detector will be about as much use as a willow wand.'

'We believe they are of the metal type.'

'Believing's not good enough. I like having feet on the ends of my legs.'

'I am sure that Pablo would know.'

'If he does, well and good. If he's not sure, it's off.'

'But we've made all arrangements!' he said.

'Look, I don't give a bugger about your arrangements. There's always another day.'

Fischer sighed. 'It will be such a pity.'

'It'd be more of a pity,' I said, 'if my dogs were left without their daddy.'

'Dogs? I don't understand . . .'

'No, well, you wouldn't, would you. Anyway,' I went on, 'that's the way it's going to be. What's your pro-gramme tomorrow night?'

'I shall cast off from here at 0021.'

'What time will you leave your house?'

'Not later than 2300.'

'That's fine. If you haven't heard from me by then, it's all systems go.'

'Will you speak to Herr Harvester in the meantime?'

'You bet I will,' I said. 'Leave that side of things to

me.' Mackenzie was hefting and sighting the rifle, trying it out for feel. I turned to him. 'You satisfied, Jock?'

'Quite. It's a nice piece,' he said.

'Right then, get it back in its box, and let's be on our way.'

As Mackenzie was dismantling the rifle I reached for the carton of shells and slipped it into my raincoat pocket. Fischer had been smoking his foul cigarettes all night but, now, as I fired a pipe, he had the gall to open a side-screen. From the ten-metre yacht whose high white freeboard loomed over our starboard side there came the sounds of great jollity. Throbbing pop-music, high-pitched chat, and the screeching laughter of girls. The big yawl moored to port had looked to be dark and deserted, her hatches battened tight and her sails neatly reefed and lashed in their covers.

'One other thing, Fischer,' I said, 'when you push off tomorrow night, you're going to attract some attention.'

'You forget, Herr Stroud,' he said, 'that at 0020 they'll lose all power.'

'Yes, I know,' I said, 'but the Voppos have night-glasses, don't they?'

'Undoubtedly,' he said, 'but they will have much else to be thinking about – and the *Inga* is hard to see.'

On a moonless night, it would be of course. Mackenzie's sideways glance told me he thought I was picking at nits, and I had to admit to myself he was right. In the context of the overall plan, Fischer's role was least open to question. Getting Jagersberg off the beach really wasn't his pigeon, and there was no point in wittering on. The people to get at were Pablo and Harvester. I pushed myself up off the bunk, taking care this time to duck my head.

'Ready, Jock?' He picked up the gun case, and nodded. 'Right, you go first,' I said. 'I haven't another pair of dry socks.'

65

As he opened the cabin door a swirling cloud of smoke billowed out, much of it rank and stale, left over from the afternoon session. I let him get off the pontoon, and nodded at Fischer.

'I'll say goodbye, then.'

'No,' he said, 'say *aufwiedersehen*.'

'Yes, well, I hope you're right, chum.'

The Germans are great boys for shaking hands. He pumped my fist again, and I joined Mackenzie up on the jetty. The shindig on the yacht alongside appeared to be reaching a swinging climax. All its side-screen curtains were drawn, and judging from the excited screeches, it was perhaps as well that they were. The music had been turned up louder, and water slapped hard at her hull as the whole boat rocked on her moorings.

'Some party,' Mackenzie said.

I looked across at the opposite shore. It was quiet as the grave, the only sign of life being the dull shaded glow from the spaced-out watchtowers. The contrast was ominously depressing. I had a premonition of doom. We set off along the esplanade, back towards the hotel, and walked for several minutes in silence. Then:

'I've a feeling, Mackenzie,' I said, 'that you think I was hard on Fischer.'

'No, not really,' he said.

'Don't you dissemble with me, lad, or I'll kick your arse back home.'

'You did rather seem to be *looking* for snags.'

'That's the name of this game, and you'd better bear that well in mind if you're set on a long career.'

'Oh, I am!'

'The pension's pretty lousy.'

'I know, and I don't mind,' he said.

'No, I don't suppose you need to. But tell me – did Fischer strike you as odd?'

'Odd? In what way?'

'No particular way. What's your feeling about the man?'

'Well, he did seem a little bit . . . nervous . . .?'

'Anxious?'

'Yes, that's a better word.'

'Why should a freelance be anxious? Why should Fischer *care*?' I was talking more to myself than Mackenzie.

'He probably just needs the cash.'

My instinct would not let me buy that, but: 'Maybe. We'll see,' I said.

'What's on the menu tomorrow?'

'An early start,' I said. 'I want you to run me down to Lübeck to get the five past six train. It gets into Hamburg at five to seven. The Berlin train leaves at eight, and I want to see Harvester before I catch it.'

'What shall I do the rest of the day?'

'Just keep a low profile,' I said, 'practise not attracting attention. I've given you Harvester's private number. Anything untoward, get in touch with me through him.'

'Roger. Got it,' he said.

When we collected our keys from the porter we fixed early-morning calls. Then, as we crossed the lobby towards the lifts, we heard from the residents' bar a lively hum of late-night revelry. I didn't want to go to bed.

'Listen, Mackenzie – how's about a night-cap?'

'Er . . . I won't, if you don't mind,' he said. 'But I'll keep you company, if you like.'

'Oh, to hell with it,' I said.

'No, come on, I'll have a coffee.'

'That would put me right off,' I said. 'Christ, lad, you're worse than Charlie McGowan. No, I'll have a drink in my room.'

In the continental fashion, rooms at the Maritim were equipped with a nice little cabinet stocked with miniatures of booze, and a good selection of mixes. I helped myself to a Scotch, and when I'd poured it, I didn't really want it. I set it beside the bed, and got on the blower to Harvester's office. The night man was good at his job, and patched me through in a matter of seconds. Harvester seemed wide awake, and without asking any stupid questions, quickly agreed to the meet. I stripped off my clothes and padded naked into the bathroom to wash, and clean my teeth. As I was scouring away the smoke-stains I noticed three small complementary sachets of Badedas on the end of the bath, by the taps. I filled the tub and dumped in the lot and soaked in the fragrant suds until the water began to cool. Then, after a brisk rub down, I puffed through a short course of exercises before turning in with *The Little Sister*. But I didn't read for long. Chandler's prose seemed to lack the old magic. My bad leg had started to ache, a sure sign of something or other.

With luck, it only meant rain.

Saturday

'Very interesting,' Harvester mused.

'I'm glad you think so,' I said. 'They damn' nearly took my head off.'

'And you've no idea who they were?'

'Yobs. Who they were doesn't matter – who hired them's what I'd like to know.'

'Someone who wants you out of the running.'

'That much is obvious,' I said.

'I'll put out some feelers.'

'Do that. Any new cousins in town?'

'None that we know of.'

'Can't you find out?'

'It might take some little time.'

'Better check the MOSSAD boys, too.'

'What makes you – '

'Nothing,' I said. 'It's just a gut-feeling.'

'Very well. Anything else I can do?'

'Can you organize a car to the station?'

'Yes, you mustn't miss that train or you'll never get to the football match. Incidentally, Fischer tells me you asked for a rifle.'

'Oh, does he, now?' I said.

'Yes, he does, and I'm not sure it's wise. The last thing we want to see is a messy border incident.'

'Really? Well, the last thing *I* want to see is some corner of a foreign field.'

'Oh, come now – '

'Don't give me that! I've got this feeling in my water, had it all along.'

'Female intuition?'

'Call it what you like. It's something I picked up from Charlie McGowan.'

'Pity he's on the sick list.'

'You can bloodywell say that again. If he wasn't, I wouldn't be arsing around with a blushing raw recruit and a double I wouldn't want to trust with my laundry.'

'I've told you, Farrow,' he said, 'that Fischer has proven his worth to us, and that Pablo is one of our own.'

'I know damn well what you told me. But something about this job stinks – '

We were interrupted at that point by a discreet knock on the door, and a middle-aged woman entered. She was balancing a tray, and edged past me in that tiny office to set it down on the desk. It smelled like real fresh-ground coffee.

'Thank you, Joan,' Harvester said.

The woman nodded, and left us, closing the door at her back.

'Cup of coffee before you go?'

'Might as well,' I said.

'Sugar and milk?'

'Just sugar. Listen – '

'No, *you* listen, Farrow,' he said. The fat man had not raised his voice, but something in his tone made me shut my mouth and hear him out. 'They told me,' he went on, 'that you were an awkward customer, and apparently they were right. They also told me, however, that in the absence of Charles McGowan you were the best available man. I must say I'm beginning to doubt that.'

'Are you, though?' I said. 'So what are you going to do about it?'

'Nothing. It's too late,' he said. 'This operation is too far advanced, and it's taken a lot of hard work to set it up satisfactorily.'

'Satisfactorily!' I said.

'Yes. We believe in Pablo implicitly. If he says it's going to work – '

'All right,' I broke in, 'you can spare me the rest. What about this car?'

'You haven't drunk your coffee yet.'

'You can have two cups,' I said.

The train to Berlin was pretty full, but I bagged a corner seat and began to read the front page of *Die Welt*. Or as much of it as I could. Speaking German is one thing, but reading it is something else. Once we were nicely out of the station I went along to the restaurant car and ordered up a proper breakfast. The waiter wasn't too happy about it. He said there would be some delay. I told him I didn't mind about that, and to bring me a pot of tea. I should have stuck with the rolls and jam. The bacon, when it came, was almost unrecognizable and the scrambled eggs were cold and the sausages were plastic horrors. But the big crisp rolls were good, and I ate four with plenty of creamy butter.

I had almost finished the meal when the train slowed down to enter a small, dreary station. I could not see any sign, but I knew we were at the border by the Voppo uniforms. There were scores of them, strung out all along the platform. They swarmed aboard the train, three or four to every entrance, as though intending to take it by storm. Every one of them was armed with a pistol, and the latest MPiKM, and I hadn't any doubt that all were loaded. I suddenly became aware that an uncanny hush had fallen upon the dining car. All chattering had ceased, and people had even stopped eating. The waiters had disappeared. It was a curiously chilling experience.

'You there – stay where you are!'

The 'you' was a child of seven or eight who had been sitting across the gangway from me beside an attractive young woman. The little girl had stepped away from her

71

seat in order to look down the carriage and see what was going on. The young woman grabbed the child's arm, and pulled her back with a hiss of reproach. I fished out my Herbert Stroud passport, ready for when they came. It took them a long time to get to me. The train was well under way, speeding through flat, uninteresting country populated only by cows which seemed to belong to no one. No passenger made a move, and no one spoke unless spoken to by the Voppo inquisitors. They had started at one end of the carriage. I was halfway along, with the back of my head towards them. I forebore from turning round, because it didn't seem to be the done thing. Finally, my turn came.

'Passport!'

Three of them. One to inspect, and two to intimidate. Slung by a broad leather strap around the neck of the one doing the inspecting was a sort of cinema usherette's tray, loaded with paraphernalia. Various printed pads, and rubber stamps, and God knows what else. He was thorough, to say the least. He examined every page of my passport, and then he examined me.

'What is the purpose of this visit?'

The way he said it suggested that, no matter what I said, he wasn't going to believe me. He was a stocky, whey-faced character with those very pale brown eyes never to be trusted in man or beast and especially not in a dog. I put on a definite English accent.

'I am going straight through Berlin.'

'What is the purpose of this visit!'

'All right, tourist,' I said.

'Luggage?'

'None. I return this evening.'

He stared at me as though he hoped I was lying, and I knew he was going to check. But he banged a blue and yellow entry stamp in my passport and tossed it back at me and I only just managed to catch it. Then the trio turned round to the woman and child, and so on slowly down the car. No one moved until several minutes after they had finally gone. Then I joined the orderly exodus and made my way up the train, back to my own compartment. Voppos stationed at each end of every corridor stood with their backs to the doors, machine-pistols slung at the horizontal ready. Anybody mad enough to jump off a speeding train would first need to smash a window, and by that time he would be dead.

The old man who had been sitting next to me was having his suitcase searched, and his motley possessions were heaped on my seat. So I stood outside in the corridor until the Voppos were through with him. These were a different crew, so there must, I realized, be a separate five-man team assigned to every car. Exactly what they hoped to find was anybody's guess. Probably nothing. Harassment is a most effective deterrent, and if there's one thing the Others hate it's traffic into West Berlin.

The next place at which we stopped reminded me of wartime Crewe, except that it was even more depressing. No one got off, and no one got on. The bare and empty station itself seemed incidental to the sprawl of marshalling yards, and the huddle of soot-grimed brick warehouses. But the utter drabness of the scene was ameliorated by the majestic presence of four or five huge old locomotives splendidly shrouded in steam which spurted and hissed from stacks and escape-valves. When I craned forward to get a better sight of them, the old man touched my arm.

'The only beautiful things left here,' he whispered.

When I turned round to agree with him, he hurriedly looked away and buried his nose in his newspaper.

That halt must have been at a signal, because soon we were moving again and the next stop we made was at Staaken, at the border with West Berlin. Here, the Voppos piled off to form ranks on the platform. No

73

passengers disembarked, and then we were passing slowly through Spandau. It was possible to see parts of the grim fortress prison, and I thought of its solitary inmate. What a stupid waste. Nobody seemed to be sharing my thoughts. Normality was restored, and people were laughing and talking again. As we rolled into the clean, airy station overlooking the zoo, luggage was hauled down off the racks. Having none to worry about, I was one of the first to step down. The big station clock said eleven-fifty-five. We were almost half an hour late.

Although I wasn't hungry, I decided to have some lunch before I went any further. I ate in one of the station snack bars. Hardly a gourmet's delight, but food was the least of my worries. I persevered with the meal only because I had no idea where, or when, I might get the next one.

A ticket from Am Zoo to Friedrichstrasse, the S-bahn station at Checkpoint Charlie, costs rather more than a ticket from Victoria to Brixton, but is just as easy to buy. That is where any similarity ends. Although the German train is less dirty, it has bone-jarring wooden seats, and the wheels, if not square, are elliptical. Then, there's the infamous Wall, and no one who has never actually seen it can imagine quite what it's like. As we made our jolting approach I marvelled that escapers should even attempt the feat, and the knowledge that a few had done so successfully made me view the prospects at Travemunde in a new and less off-putting light. The station itself was a maze of bare corridors connected by long flights of stairs, and the human traffic was strictly one-way. There were Voppos everywhere. I let myself be borne along by the mute shuffling stream of humanity which gradually, by a succession of barriers and turnstiles, was reduced to a disorientated single-file crawl. The crawl became a silent queue which inched its way past a half-glassed cubicle. The cubicle had a breast-high sliding window with, standing behind it, a uniformed Voppo.

'Passport,' he said, 'and remove the glasses.'

I took off the big dark shades, and handed him my Herbert Stroud passport. He studied my damaged face, apparently comparing it feature by feature with the passport photograph. When he was sure that I was me, he pointed with one corner of the passport at my nicely healing eye.

'What was the nature of this injury?'

'As a matter of fact,' I said, 'I was hit by a flying champagne cork.'

That drew a baleful glare, and I instantly regretted the quip.

'So. We shall see,' he said.

He turned round to one of his buddies seated behind a grey steel desk, and tossed down my passport and muttered something. I couldn't quite catch what he said, but the buddy looked up at me, and nodded. Me and my big mouth. The first one came back to his window, slapped down a printed form, and dismissed me with a sideways jerk of his head. I followed the arrow signs down yet another bleak corridor and pushed through a pair of swing doors and found myself in a vast grim chamber whose high walls were painted dark brown. The floor was of uncovered concrete, worn smooth by an endless procession of feet. I was taken aback by the number of people scattered all over the place. There must have been five or six hundred of them, many more than had got off the train, and for a moment I wondered where they'd all come from. Then it dawned on me. They were passengers from previous trains. There were no chairs or benches, nowhere to sit. They stood around in loose, silent groups, waiting dispiritedly. There was a crushing atmosphere of dumb resignation and soul-numbing apathy. Many of them were elderly, and most were modestly dressed. I guessed they would be visiting relatives living behind the Wall, sons and daughters and grandchildren. Some were still filling in their forms, and I felt for a pen to fill in my own.

Much of the information called for was recorded in my passport, but I knew there was no way out of it so I wrote it all down again. I listed how much money I was carrying, what the currencies were, and how much of it I intended to convert into East German marks. I noted my time of arrival, forecast the time I'd depart, and recorded my mother's maiden name and the town in which she was born. Most of the questions were patently farcical, designed to irritate. Suddenly, as I was scribbling away, I heard the crackle of a switched-on loudspeaker. The hush intensified. There was an expectant stirring, a raising of heads. The distorted message boomed out harshly, very rapid-fire, just a string of multi-digit numbers. Eight or nine of the waiting hundreds broke away from the throng, and hurried up to a small barred ticket-window set into one of the walls. I moved across to see what was happening and then, of course, I knew. The numbers called out were passport numbers, and the owners formed a line at the window clutching their filled-in forms and little bundles of money. They were dealt with one by one, and straggled away through an open door in a corner of the hall. When the last person moved away from the window it was closed with a peremptory crash, and the crowd settled down to do some more waiting.

I made another quick estimate of the number of people there. Christ, this was going to take all day. I looked at my watch again. It was very nearly ten minutes to two, and the kick-off was at three, and there seemed just no way I was going to make it. At this rate, I'd be lucky to get to the stadium before the final whistle blew. Another thought struck me. I didn't know my passport number. There was only one thing to do. I stationed myself by the barred window, and leaned against the wall. The window was backed by a wooden counter on which stood a microphone, and sitting in front of the microphone on a typist's swivel chair was a dumpy, sullen-faced female Voppo. By her right hand, a wire filing basket lay under the mouth of a chute, and at widely irregular intervals a bundle of passports rattled down the chute and fell with a flop in the tray. Then the woman would switch on her mike, reel off the numbers just once, and slide back the window. Open for business.

And what a business it was. Every passive supplicant was submitted yet again to a slow, deliberate scrutiny before his or her passport was handed over. They were also handed a heat-sealed transparent envelope containing the equivalent in East German currency, at the lousy official rate, of ten West German marks. This was the compulsory minimum exchange without which no one was allowed to enter. But the extortion did not end there. Each West German national living in West Berlin was made to pay a five-mark entry fee. It added up to a nice little racket, and I wondered why they didn't cash in more efficiently by speeding things up a bit. Maybe they couldn't make up their minds which they wanted most – the money, or to make things so difficult that people wouldn't want to come.

As an exercise to pass the time, and to take my mind off my aching leg, I tried to spot a pattern in the rate at which the batches of passports came tumbling down into the tray. After watching carefully for more than an hour, I decided there wasn't one. They arrived in lots of between five and a dozen and once I counted thirteen. At three o'clock I reckoned that something like eighty-odd people had been summoned up to the window, but the total number left in the hall had actually grown. The stream coming in had far surpassed the trickle moving out. The dreary performance was sad and depressing, and to make matters even worse, it simply wasn't permitted to give in and call it a day. Once in that hall you were caught in the system, and there was only one way to go. You waited until they let you in. Then, before they let you out, you were made to suffer it all again.

So I stood there, trying to think calm thoughts and forget my aching thigh. Tobacco would have helped a lot, but I daren't light a pipe because nobody else was smoking, and I didn't want to risk a scene. Time dragged on and, finally, the familiar blue and gold passport thudded into the tray. What were the words? *Without let or hindrance.* What a bloody joke. I let an old couple go before me. My turn at the window then, and the woman just stared for what seemed like minutes. She did it with never a blink, and I'd seen warmer eyes on a long-dead fish. In the end, when she was ready:

'Fifteen marks,' she said.

'But I'm a British tourist,' I said, 'I need to pay only ten.'

'Fifteen marks,' she said again.

I knew I was going to have to let her win, because if I didn't, I'd be there for ever. I wouldn't have minded so much had I thought the slab-faced little bitch was on the fiddle, but there was no doubt in my mind that the extra five marks she screwed out of me would go straight into party funds. So I swallowed my bile and paid up meekly and got the hell out of there.

I was faced, outside of Friedrichstrasse station, with a cheerless, lacklustre world. The long straight road was dismally worse than the worst of the backside of Leeds. It was flanked by tall dreary buildings, long blocks of featureless flats with unpainted windows and pitted façades. No colour anywhere. No billboards, no gay advertisements, not one single neon sign. A curious absence of traffic, and very few people about. Nothing which looked like a taxi. Directly opposite the station, a

78

bus stop, with a sorry-looking queue. Striding towards me, a youth in an anorak.

'Excuse me, son,' I said, 'could you tell me the way to the stadium, please?'

He did not answer me but he turned round, still walking on, to point back the way he had come. I saw them then, the tall steel lattices of floodlight gantries. They towered above the intervening rooftops, perhaps a mile away. There was still no sign of a taxi, so I set off briskly to walk. It was almost a quarter past four, and the game would be well into the second half. My contact would be doing his nut. I covered the distance as fast as I could without breaking into a trot, but the gantries were further away than they seemed and it took me a good twenty minutes to reach the football ground. Then I had to find the correct turnstile for entry to stand number three. The elderly man who took my ticket gave me an old-fashioned look, but by that time I was well past caring. I hurried along the back of the stand, with the roar of the crowd in my ears, and started to climb the deserted stairs. The flights were very steep, and they seemed to zigzag upwards for ever. Row 'A' was at the back, and seat number twenty was on the aisle. Now I knew what had happened to all the people. The stadium was packed, and the crowd was in a state of high excitement. The scoreboard said two all.

The man in seat number twenty-one was crouched forward, elbows on knees. When I sat down, panting, he glanced sideways and nodded his head and handed me a red and white scarf like the one he was wearing himself. Him and most of the other spectators. The colours of East Berlin. I draped the scarf around my neck, and tucked the ends into my coat.

'Sorry I'm late. I got held up.'

'Yes, I thought you might be,' he said. 'Pity. It's been a very good game.'

79

He was one of those faceless characters very hard to describe, seen and instantly forgotten a hundred times a day. Mousy brown hair and mousy brown eyes in a face neither fat nor thin and with no distinguishing features. Medium height and medium build, medium everything. He was wearing a mud-coloured belted raincoat, cheap black moulded shoes, and dull grey slacks with turn-ups. When he spoke, his lips hardly moved. He kept his eyes on the game.

'Did you have any trouble?'

'Nothing unusual.'

'Good. It's all arranged.'

'Listen – '

'No,' he said, 'later.'

Although he showed no outward sign of excitement, he seemed intent on the match. The home team was mounting a desperate attack, and when in the last few minutes they scored to go one goal ahead, supporters gave vent to their feelings in the usual time-honoured way. My companion merely leaned back in his seat.

'That seems to be it, then,' I said. 'So what about getting out of here, before we get caught in the rush?'

People all around us had leaped up on to their feet, waving scarves and yelling so loudly I barely heard his reply.

'The "rush",' he said, 'is why we are here.'

Of course, and I ought to have known. By himself, he was inconspicuous. I was anything but, and together we made a very odd couple. We needed the sheltering throng. So we waited for the final whistle, then merged with the jostling mob in the rush for stairways and exits. Very few seemed to have cars, and we lost ourselves in the the noisy procession streaming out of the ground to wind its way towards Friedrichstrasse. We passed the station there, and trudged on down that dismal road almost to its end. As it straggled on past junctions and side-roads, the crowd began to disperse. We stayed with a large contingent which broke away to the left, and found ourselves entering a big smoky beer joint which quickly became very crowded as more and more fans pressed in. I took off my glasses and kept my mouth shut and followed Pablo's lead to sit on a bench at a long wooden table, up at its furthermost end.

There were good-natured shouts for service, and the waiters who bustled around wore long white aprons down to their ankles. Pablo asked for two beers, and said something else which I didn't quite catch. The place was a bedlam of sound. When at last our sweating waiter fought his way back through the crush, I saw what it was that Pablo had ordered. Apart from two mugs of beer, a communal platter of bread and sliced sausage. When Pablo had paid the man, he slid the piled-up plate between us.

'Better eat something,' he said.

I didn't really want any food, but I knew it was sound advice. The leathery sausage was stinking with garlic, a flavouring I never could stand, and the coarse black bread was served without butter. I swilled the stuff down with ale, and managed to get through my half of it. The sausage made me burp, and I lit a pipe in a fruitless effort to kill the lingering taste. We appeared to be with the noisy party of more than a dozen strong, and nobody took any notice of us. Pablo turned aside once or twice to swap words with the man on his left, but mostly he talked to me and we talked about nothing but football.

As the rowdy evening wore on, I began to feel progressively anxious. Four of our number had left the table, to a chorus of drunken goodbyes, and others were making departure noises. The crowd was thinning out fast and with it, of course, our camouflage. I sneaked a glance at my watch. It was twenty past seven and surely, I thought, time we were on our way. I nudged Pablo's elbow.

'It's getting late.'

'Yes, I know,' he said, 'but there's plenty of time. Don't worry.'

So I nursed the dregs of my beer, aching now to get on with it. Another ten minutes dragged by, then two of the men further down at our table drank off and got up to go. Pablo's foot tapped my ankle, and we followed them to the door, as though the four of us were leaving together. It was almost dark outside, and the street we were in was poorly lit. The night was decidedly cool, and I tucked the scarf up around my neck. We casually followed our unwitting friends, tagging along at their heels until we came to the wide main road. When they veered tipsily left at the corner, we crossed and turned to the right, heading back up towards Friedrichstrasse. But we did not walk very far before Pablo led off on a cobbled side-street lined with little shops, none of which had its window lit up.

'Not very far, now,' he said.

The car, a dilapidated Lada 1300, was parked along with several others on a weed-ridden square of waste ground between a pair of tall dark gables. Pablo unlocked his door, then leaned across the car to open mine. I quickly ducked inside and the engine, which sounded strong and healthy, responded to the starter first time. Pablo hunched forward to switch on the sidelights, and then we were away.

'Jesus,' I said, 'what a racket back there. I was glad to get out of the place.'

'It was somewhere safe to pass the time.'

'Maybe, but talking of time,' I said, 'I'd say we were dangerously short of it, now.'

'No, not really,' he said. 'Don't be deceived by appearances. This car runs extremely well, and I am a very good driver.'

'Oh, I believe you,' I said, 'but if I remember rightly, Schonberg's a hundred and thirty miles away.'

'Don't worry, we'll be there by 2230.'

'Even so,' I said, 'it'll still be a very damn near-run thing. I was hoping there'd be time for discussion.'

He was using the city's back-doubles, driving fast along near-empty streets which skirted the main arterial thoroughfares. When we picked up the autobahn signs I was seized by an awful dull feeling. A sense of being manipulated, a prisoner in the car. Most of my fellow day-visit entrants would be leaving just about now, and I knew that the Voppos at Friedrichstrasse would soon be starting to wonder what had happened to me. I reckoned I had about an hour before they began to check up, and if I hadn't made my exit by nine o'clock . . .

'Hey! Bloody slow down, mate!' I said. 'I want you to convince me that this job's properly laid on. Otherwise, you can take me back – '

'It is too late, my friend,' he said. 'Too many wheels have been set in motion. If we do not take Jagersberg now, we shall never get another chance.'

He gunned the car on to an autobahn approach road, and as we roared up the ramp, I knew we were past the point of return. But:

'Don't push me, Pablo,' I said, 'because if you do, I might just surprise you!'

'Please, be calm,' he said. 'I promise you that all will go well.'

The little man was calm enough for both of us. He handled the Lada with skill, and I quickly realized the car had been doctored. It wasn't what it seemed. We were overtaking everything.

'All right, then,' I said, 'fill me in on the detail.'

'Ah, that's better!' he said. 'Now – what do you know about lasers?'

'Bugger-all,' I said. 'I'm just a simple country boy.'

'I can hardly believe that,' he said, 'but let me tell you something more about them. It will help you to understand how vitally important it is to move Herr Jagersberg . . .' I settled back against the squab, resigned now to seeing it through, and listened as Pablo raised his voice above the engine's burgeoning growl. Part of what he told me I already knew, but I let him ramble on. '. . . so the Russians began to experiment in 1974 with attempts to interfere with the US Nathan Hale spy satellites. They perfected a very highly complicated system of heat sensors to detect the infra-red radiation from launchings, then tried to beam in on the missiles as they embarked upon first orbit. Those early efforts were not successful, because beyond a certain level of projection, their laser beams encountered what is now known as "thermal bloom" – a phenomenon which occurs when coherent energy transforms the atmosphere through which it passes into an ionised plasma. This impedes the passage of the beam, and reduces its force to way below MHPL.'

'Just a minute,' I said, 'what's MHPL?'

'Mean Hull Penetration Level.'

'You mean the beam would just bounce off?'

He nodded, hunching over the wheel. 'Anyway,' he went on, 'it was realized then that, with the existing technology, laser warfare was possible only in outer space. Unfortunately, the cumbersome power-plants and generator converters required to produce effective laser emissions are so huge and complicated as virtually to preclude their being set up in space. Also, they would be very vulnerable.'

'So what came next?' I said.

'Next came PALDEW – Particle-Loaded Direct Energy Weapon, the brainchild of Jagersberg.'

'So what makes PALDEW different?'

'Everything,' Pablo said. 'Jagersberg got the idea of introducing sub-atomic particles into the laser beam. Not

84

only would this eliminate the nuisance of thermal bloom, it would greatly increase the MHPL.'

'They've got it made, then,' I said.

'Not quite. There's still much work to be done. However, the imbalance of know-how between East and West has narrowed most dangerously.'

'What about the Helsinki SALT talks, last June?'

'Just a lot of ballyhoo, with both sides feeling their way. Everybody knows that arms control doesn't mean a thing unless it includes Direct Energy Weapons. The next war will be in space, and all conventional hardware is completely useless up there. Explosions – even atomic explosions – have no effect whatever in the blast-proof vacuum of space. The laser is the weapon of the future, and of course the future is *now*.'

'But the politicians keep on saying it's all Buck Rogers stuff. Technologically impossible.'

Pablo snorted derisively. 'Don't you believe it,' he said. 'ASAT is a fact of life, and when they link it with GPS – '

'Hang on a minute, you've lost me now.'

'Sorry. I'll start with GPS. This is a system of computer plug-in which allows ICBM missiles to be directed – and even re-directed after launching – on any target, however small, which walks or crawls or slithers anywhere on earth. ASAT means Anti-Satellite.'

'Which in turn means laser beams.'

'Which now means *particle-charged* laser beams.'

'So put the two together and . . . Jesus Christ!' I said, 'what a monumental waste of human endeavour. The whole bloody thing's obscene!'

'Obscene or not,' he said mildly, 'the US has already spent more than two billion dollars on ASAT research, and has voted to spend the same again.'

'My God – that's two thousand billion quid!'

'Yes. So now you can see why Jagersberg simply must be got out.'

'How did our lot first latch on to the old boy?'

'With respect, that is not your concern. However, if you're going to insist – '

'Forget it. I don't want to know.' We had just passed the exit for Havelburg, and an illuminated sign which said *Ludwigslust 70 km*. This was where we would leave the main Berlin–Hamburg autobahn and turn away due north for the short last lap up to Schonberg. Another eighty or ninety minutes' driving should just about see us there. I couldn't turn back now if I wanted to, because where the hell would I go? So: 'What I do want to know,' I went on, 'is exactly what happens after Schonberg.'

'Didn't Fischer tell you?'

'Yes, he did,' I said, 'but let's hear it straight from the horse's mouth.'

He shrugged his narrow shoulders, both hands gripping the wheel and his unblinking stare on the road ahead. 'Fair enough,' he said. 'When we get to the cottage – '

'Will Jagersberg be alone?'

'Oh, yes. One of the local women comes in each day to clean and cook and so on, but she goes home after she's given him his supper.'

'What about neighbours?' I said.

'The house is on the outskirts of the village. Jagersberg's nearest neighbour is a hundred metres away.'

'You're sure the cottage isn't watched?'

'Absolutely,' he said. 'Anyway, he's been warned there must be no delay, so when we get there he will be ready and waiting. He will carry nothing, of course, and – '

'No papers?'

'His "papers" are all in his head.'

'Then I hope he's got a good memory. Go on.'

'You are familiar with the Ost Strand terrain?'

'Well, I've studied the map.'

'Then you'll know that the beach is backed by dunes.'

'Yes. Any mines there?' I said.

'No, because Voppos from the married quarters often picnic there. The only mines you have to worry about are between the watchtowers and the sea, and we're pretty sure we know a safe path. Two or three weeks ago we watched a maintenance party working on the boom. They go to it by heading along a dead straight line between tower number one and the point at which the sea-barrier joins the border fence.'

'Maybe, but that was in daylight I take it?'

'There are night-glasses in the boot. Also inflatable life-jackets, and a mine-detector. All right?'

'All right,' I said, 'but talking of mines, do you know what type they are?'

'Don't worry, Herr Stroud, they are metal-cased. They've been there for several years. Anyway, I will drive you to a spot near the barracks, about three kilometres back from the beach. From there, of course, you must go in on foot.'

'What about patrols?'

'There are patrols,' he admitted, 'but the Voppos have grown very lax. There has never been an incident up there.'

'Until tonight, you mean. Fischer said something about diversions.'

'That's correct. Oh, and by the way' – he leaned forward to switch on the dashboard radio – 'you'd better check your watch against local time. There'll be a signal coming up soon.'

'What sort of capers have you laid on, then?'

'First, and most important, there's the power station at Wismar.'

87

'I know about that,' I said. 'It's supposed to break down at twenty past midnight.'

'It's supposed to, and it will. And the standby generator at the Voppo barracks has already been sabotaged.'

'Don't they ever give it a test run?'

'Oh, yes, every Monday,' he said. 'It was put out of action yesterday. Now the motor will not start.'

'That's comforting,' I said. 'But Fischer implied there'd be other distractions.'

'Yes. The guard in the towers is changed at midnight. Transports leave the barracks at 2350, and reach the access-road terminals about 2355. From there, the new guard – two to each tower – have a five minute walk down the beach. The transports wait at the terminals for the men who have been relieved, and take them back to the barracks.'

'Christ, all that bloody activity right at the crucial time!'

'We feel it will serve as useful cover. Think about it,' he said.

I thought about it for all of ten seconds. 'Perhaps you're right,' I said. 'But you still haven't told me what else you've been up to.'

'I'm coming to that,' he said. 'Two of our people are standing by between towers three and four. At exactly ten past midnight, they will drive a herd of goats – '

'On to the beach?'

'You've got it.'

'Bloody hard lines on the goats.'

'Would you rather we used people?'

'All right, what else?' I said.

'Nothing. That's it. When the mines begin to explode, you should be at the boom, ready to enter the water.'

'You make it sound easy, but what if we're spotted?'

A stupid question. He glanced at me. 'You can only go forward,' he said.

Suddenly the heat in the car was oppressive. I wound my window part down, and let in a rush of cold fresh air. We drove on in silence for quite some time, me with my sombre thoughts. Soft music from the radio, a Beethoven symphony. When the lights of Wittenburg faded behind us we soon raised the Ludwigslust sign, and Pablo began to slow down for the turn-off. The road he took to the north carried two-way traffic, but not very much. It ran through a forest of pines. The Beethoven ended, and I checked my watch with the pips, but it needed no adjustment. A news reader launched on his spiel, but I could not concentrate on it. The tarmac road punched an endless black tunnel through the overhanging trees. Four or five miles into the forest, Pablo touched my arm.

'There is a pistol in the door-pocket.'

A Walther PPK, with a full magazine and one up the spout.

'There should be a silencer, too.'

I groped around in the bottom of the pocket, and found it, and hauled it out.

'What's this in aid of?'

'I don't really think we're going to be stopped, but if we are,' he replied, 'we must deal with whoever stops us. We can't let them search the car.'

'Christ, all they need do is ask for my papers.' I was fumbling with the heavy silencer, trying to match the thing with the newly turned thread on the end of the barrel. It didn't want to play. PPKs don't take kindly to silencers, they are not built for the job. Pablo glanced across at my efforts.

'Is something wrong?'

I had finally forced the threads to marry. 'No, it's all right,' I said. 'A spot of oil would have helped, though.'

'Good. If we *are* stopped, get out of the car and shoot before they realize what's happening.'

'You can bank on it, mate,' I said.

But we travelled all the way into Schonberg without seeing another car. Pablo tooled slowly through the village, which at half past ten on this Saturday night was quiet as the grave. The hamlet lay in a gentle hollow, bisected by a stream and surrounded by hills clad thickly with pines. We drove straight through on spotlight only so I didn't see much of the place beyond a vague huddle of old-looking houses, the lych-gate of a church, and a garage with a couple of hand-cranked pumps. Halfway up a steepish hill going out on the other side, Pablo took a sudden sharp turning on to a narrow dirt road which cut through the trees at a rising angle. Then, a white-painted fence, and he swung us into a short curved drive-way. I had one brief glimpse of a windowless gable before he snapped off the spot, and set the handbrake and killed the engine. We sat there listening to soft ticking noises as the souped-up power-plant cooled.

'This is it,' my companion said. 'Do you wish to come inside?'

'Why not. Let's have a look at the bloke.'

We eased ourselves out of the car. I was holding the pistol, with my thumb on the safety catch. In the tiny glow from the courtesy light, just before I closed my door, I saw Pablo pass round the front of the car. He paused by the bonnet, listening and waiting. I groped my way forward in the darkness, and felt his hand on my arm. The air was chill. I could smell the pines. We stood there in front of the car, feeling the heat from its radiator. My eyes began to adjust, and then I could make out the bulk of the cottage looming against the stars. Pablo either had eyes like a cat, or he knew his way around. He led me as though he was guiding a blind man, holding me close to his side, and I felt stone paving under my feet. The flagged path fronted the house, and Pablo stopped at a box-like porch to fumble at the door. He found the knob, and pushed the door open, and nudged me on inside and I sensed him step in after me. Then he closed the outer door, and brushed past me to tap on the inner one. It was warm inside the porch, but darker than it had been outside. As Pablo tapped again, we heard the sound of a bolt being drawn.

'Watch out – there's a step,' Pablo said.

A tiny squeak of hinges and a rush of really warm air, but still not so much as a glimmer of light. I stumbled on the step, and put out my free hand to feel my way. Fingers plucked at my sleeve, and drew me forward. First a doormat, then carpet under my feet. The sound of a door being closed behind me. Then the click of a switch, and I closed my eyes as the light hit them hard.

'This is Herr Stroud,' Pablo said. 'Herr Stroud – meet Professor Jagersberg.'

I transferred the awkward weight of the Walther from my right hand to my left, and reached out to take the old man's fist. It was reassuringly firm, and I was relieved to see he looked fit for his age. His bushy hair was quite dark, though his spiky eyebrows and Kaiser moustache were almost entirely grey. He was lean and stringy, and that made me happy.

'How d'you do, sir,' I said.

'I am pleased to meet you, Herr Stroud – please, come in.'

The low gloomy hall with its dark oak staircase smelled of furniture wax. As the old man motioned to a door on his right, he glanced down at the gun in my hand and I thrust it into my raincoat pocket. Because of the long bulky silencer it would not go in all the way, and the butt protruded. I let it. Jagersberg opened the door, and stood back to let me precede him. At first, I saw only the books. They lined the walls from skirting board to ceiling, were piled up in stacks on the floor, and overflowed on to chairs and tables. Then my eyes were drawn to the big open fire, and then I saw the girl. She was sitting in a chair by the fireplace. The sight of her came as a shock, and she smiled as it registered on my face.

'*Guten Abend, mein Herr.*'

I turned to Pablo, standing behind me. 'What the hell's going on here?' I said.

Unless he was an extremely good actor he was every bit as startled as me. He rounded on Jagersberg. '*Verdammte Scheisse!*'

'Please . . . my daughter – ' Jagersberg said.

'Never mind your daughter – what do you think you're on?'

The old man raised his hands, palms outwards. 'It is all quite simple,' he said. 'Ilse is going with us.'

'That's what *you* think,' I said.

'My God, Herr Stroud, I swear to you – '

'Swear away, Pablo,' I said. 'Whose bloody bright idea was this?'

Jagersberg answered for him. 'Mine alone,' he said. 'Your friend knew nothing of this arrangement.'

'What arrangement?' I said. 'There isn't any arrangement!'

'But yes,' the old man said. 'If I go, she goes. If not – ' He shrugged.

'Right, that's it, then,' I said. 'Pablo, I'm going back on my own.'

'Herr Stroud, please . . . wait . . .' he said.

'Wait, nothing,' I said, 'it's a balls-up. I knew there was something wrong!'

'At least let us talk about it.'

'Talk about what?' I said. 'Listen, old man, the talking's over.'

'Very well,' he said. He spoke with quiet dignity, and moved across the room to stand by the side of his daughter's chair.

'*Scheisse!*' Pablo said again.

Jagersberg looked at him and frowned. The girl looked

up at me. She was wearing a black woollen track-suit, obviously all set to go. I judged her to be in the middle twenties. She had short dark curly hair, and big deep-set eyes like her father's. She was built somewhat like him, too. She had a neat compact figure with small, firm breasts, and hips so slim they just missed being boyish. A waist about the size of my neck. She met my stare and nodded, as though she were reading my thoughts.

'I am a dancer, Herr Stroud,' she said, 'very fit and strong. I am also a champion swimmer.'

'Yes, that is true,' said Jagersberg, 'she could easily swim many times the distance.'

'She could easily get shot, too,' I said. 'Have you thought about that?'

'Yes, of course. We are well aware of the danger.'

'I could help you with my father. He does not swim too well.'

'She has a point there,' Pablo said quickly.

'*Please*, Herr Stroud,' the girl said.

'She is all I have left,' said Jagersberg.

'Oh, Christ, all right then,' I said.

The girl jumped up. 'You mean you will take me?'

'Yes, but listen,' I said, 'if we run into trouble, you're on your own. And you'd better not get in the way.'

Jagersberg put an arm round his daughter's shoulders. 'Thank you, Herr Stroud,' he said.

'So hadn't we better be getting on our way?'

'We have a little time,' Pablo said.

'What about a drink, then?'

'Certainly,' Jagersberg said, 'I have some rum, and some schnapps, and Scotch whisky.'

'Make mine rum,' I said. 'It'll help to keep the cold out.'

Jagersberg moved to the book-cluttered sideboard.

'Schnapps for me,' Pablo said.

'Ilse?'

'Nothing thank you, Father.'

The old man took tumblers from a cupboard in the sideboard, and set about pouring the drinks. The rum was in a flat half-flask.

'We'll take that with us,' I said.

Jagersberg smiled grimly. 'Yes, why not?' He handed us our tots, and raised his glass to make a toast. 'Here's to success!' he said.

The rum wasn't as good as Navy neaters, but it spread its heat in my gut. Pablo tossed back his schnapps as though it were water.

'Ah!' he smacked his lips. 'This is very good schnapps, Professor.'

'Have some more,' Jagersberg said.

'Not just now,' Pablo said, 'but I wouldn't mind taking the bottle, also.'

'Help yourself,' Jagersberg said. 'Take anything you want from here.'

'Thanks, just the schnapps,' Pablo said. He looked at his watch. 'Perhaps we should go now.'

'Yes, we'd better,' I said. 'You all set, Professor?'

He sighed. 'Yes, I'm ready,' he said. He took a last look around the room, sank the rest of his drink, and lifted a heavy brown roll-neck sweater from off the back of a chair. He slipped off his coat and pulled on the sweater.

'Put these on, too,' the girl said. She handed him a pair of grey woollen gloves.

'Right, let's get moving,' I said, 'before I have a change of heart.'

We went out and got in the car. Pablo backed it out of the drive, drove down the narrow lane, and turned left at the road leading out of the village. We had not gone very far when I saw the flash of oncoming headlights. Pablo glanced at me, and I slid the pistol out of my pocket and laid it on my lap. The car sped past us without slowing down, and that was the last one we saw. Pablo turned off on an unpaved track which cut a swath through the trees, driving again on spotlight only. The track was scored with deep ruts, and pitted by water-filled potholes. We were tossed around in the car, lurching and jolting in second gear.

'Sorry about this,' Pablo said, 'it's just a track the foresters use.'

That bone-jarring ride lasted twenty minutes, but it felt like more than an hour. Finally, Pablo slowed down and stopped.

'Is this it?'

'Yes,' Pablo said. 'It's too risky to take the car any further.'

The three of us piled out of the Lada, and by dint of much reversing and shunting Pablo turned it round so that it faced the way we had come. Then he got out and opened the boot, and shone a shaded flashlight inside it. There were two dark blue waistcoat-type life-jackets, a big rubber partly masked torch, and a thing which looked like a small upright Hoover. The girl helped her father into one of the jackets, and tied the tapes for him.

'You take the other jacket,' I told her.

'No, I don't need it,' she said. 'Really, I'd much rather swim without one.'

I didn't feel like arguing with her. My bad leg was playing me up, and I'd visions of taking cramp in the water. So, 'Please yourself,' I said. I laid down the Walther and took off my raincoat and put the jacket on. Pablo lifted out the detector.

'This is not heavy,' he said. 'Do you know how to use a detector, Herr Stroud?'

'Too bad if I didn't,' I said.

'It is battery-operated, and the batteries are fresh.'

'I should bloodywell hope so,' I said. I slipped the

Walther into my waistband. 'How far are we now from the dunes?'

'Under two kilometres.'

'Is this where you leave us, then?'

'No, you'd never find your way through the forest.'

'Right, lead on, then,' I said.

'From this point forward, no talking.'

We struck off into the trees, walking Indian fashion in single file. The professor trod closely on Pablo's heels, followed by the girl and, lugging the detector, I brought up the rear. It was very dark in the forest. The interlacing branches blocked out all light from the stars, and Pablo was forced to use the torch. He shone its masked beam on the ground, which was covered in a deep spongy carpet of needles and strewn with fallen cones. Low-growing pine fronds brushed at our faces. We heard small scurrying sounds and once the hoot of a hunting owl. I wondered, in the absence of landmarks, how our guide knew his way. But he must have done his homework well because he led us with hardly a pause for all of twenty minutes. Then the forest ended abruptly in a thicket of sawn-off stumps where the trees had been cut to remove the cover. Pablo switched off his torch, and now we could barely discern each other. A damp wind from off the sea carried with it a tang of ozone. Soon we were deep in the dunes, plodding through sand which dragged at our ankles and sifted into our shoes. The mine detector began to feel heavy. Pablo suddenly stopped, causing us all to barge into each other. His low whisper just reached my ears.

'We should now be very close to the road used by the Voppos,' he said. 'Please wait here while I find it.'

He vanished so quickly into the darkness I never saw him go. We were in a low depression screened by tussocks of long coarse grass, one of which made a handy cushion. The others sank down, too, and I heard the girl heave a shuddering sigh.

'You all right?'

'Yes,' she said.

I looked at the green-glowing hands of my watch. The timing had been quite good. It was seventeen minutes short of midnight. I knew we couldn't be too far out, because in the otherwise-eerie silence I could hear the low wash of the sea. Pablo seemed to be gone a long time. I looked at my watch again, and saw it had been a scant four minutes. Suddenly, the girl gripped my arm, and I heard it myself. A tiny slithering sound. I raised the Walther, and snicked off the safety. Pablo must have heard the metallic click.

'Don't shoot – it's me!' he hissed.

He scrambled down beside us, and squatted on his heels. He was breathing hard.

'Did you find it?' I whispered.

'Yes, thank God,' he said. 'Come, we must go, there isn't much time.'

We trudged through the dunes to another hollow three hundred yards away, and crouched down again to wait for the transport.

'Listen carefully now,' Pablo said, 'the guards will arrive in the next five minutes, and the path they will take to the tower is thirty metres in that direction. Don't worry, you'll see their torch. I suggest you tag along behind them, keeping as close as you dare. There will be a period of three or four minutes when they'll all be up in the tower and you, Herr Stroud, must take advantage of this turnover time to make your fix on the boom. Get as far away past the tower as you possibly can before the old guard leaves. With luck, you'll have several minutes more before the new guard settles down, by which time you should be well down the beach. Any questions?'

'Just one. How do I sight on the boom in the darkness?'

'Easy,' he replied, 'it carries a string of red warning lights. The marker buoy has one, too, so you'll have no problem in that direction.'

'Good. Here's your Walther,' I said.

'No, better keep the pistol. I don't think you're going to need it, but well, one never knows. When you reach the sea, just ditch it.'

'This is goodbye, then,' I said.

'Yes,' he said. 'Goodbye, and good luck.'

He groped for my hand, and gripped it hard. Then he shook the hands of the others before he melted away, and I found myself hoping fervently that he'd make it back to the car and get well clear before the fireworks started. I later heard that he had, but it seemed only moments after he'd gone that we heard the whine of a truck. I bellied up through the clumps of sedge and squirmed to the top of the rise, and watched the steady approach of headlights. The twin beams sliced through the night, and stopped about thirty yards away. Then the rumbling motor died, and the driver cut to sidelights. The tailboard dropped with a crash, and I could just see a couple of figures jump down. I watched them step up to the cab, and pause for a moment at the driver's window. I could not hear what was said, but one of them waved and they moved away. I slid backwards down the dune, and felt around for the mine-detector. The others jumped up on their feet and huddled near to catch my whisper.

'Stay close – stay touching, and don't even breathe! Come on, let's go,' I said.

We scrambled over the top of the dune and down the other side, making no sound in the deep, soft sand. One of the guards was carrying a hand-lamp to light their way down the beach. Suddenly, the truck's engine snarled into life.

'Down!' I hissed. 'Get down!'

We flattened as headlights raked the beach, but they swung the other way as the driver reversed to make his turn. I lay with my face in the sand until they faded away altogether and then, when I raised my head, I could see the little red eyes of his tail-lights. I got up on to my knees, and twisted towards the bobbing flashlight. The guards were still wending their way. I could hear, very faintly, their murmuring voices.

'Quickly, now!' I said.

I hurried along a parallel course, thirty yards to the side and the rear, my left arm cradling the mine-detector and the Walther in my right hand. I kept my eyes on the moving hand-lamp, angling towards it now as the guards drew nearer to their objective. The tower was built like a miniature lighthouse, its thirty-foot tapering sides topped by a dimly lit chamber with a circular balcony. I let my gaze rove across the beach and saw the lights of the boom like a ruby necklace laid out on black velvet. The girl had a hold on the bottom of my jacket, maintaining contact by touch. Her rapid, frightened breathing sounded like muffled sobs.

Now the hand-lamp was shining on the tower itself, and I saw the rungs of a metal ladder fixed to its sloping side. As the guards closed in, I increased my pace, anxious to narrow the gap as much as I could without risking detection. They reached the bottom of the ladder, and the first man began to climb. I watched him get to the top and step through the gap in the platform railing. As his oppo started to climb, I slowed and crouched. We were drawing too near. If he swung round and shone his lamp . . . I held by breath. He didn't swing round. His boot soles scraped on the rungs, and the first man up crossed the lookout platform and ducked through the access door. The instant the door closed behind the second man, I got us on our way.

We seemed, in our stumbling dash for the watchtower, to make a lot of noise and I fully expected at any moment to hear a yell of alarm and be bathed in the glare of a searchlight. Then the stuttering thuds of automatic fire and the shock of slugs tearing in. That last forty yards seemed more like four hundred, but we gained the base of the tower and crouched beneath the shelter of the platform overhang. The old man seemed to be bearing up well. I groped for the girl's right arm, and then for her hand, and gave her the Walther. I put my lips to her ear.

'Take this. If anything happens, give it back to me fast.'

I felt her nod against my face, and turned back towards the sea and took a fix on the first of the boom lights. God, it looked a mile away. My thumb found the knob on the neck of the handle and I switched the detector on. It gave off a tiny, low-pitched hum, and so long as it stayed that way we wouldn't have a thing to worry about. If the hum gave way to clicks, it would mean we had trouble.

We set off down that dark empty beach.

Sunday

What we needed now was a run of good luck. We needed the old guard to linger a while and natter with the new, and then we needed the new lot to take their time settling in. If they should make a sweep of the beach with night lenses before we reached the sea . . . I tried not to think about it.

We pressed on into the darkness, heading straight for that first red light. I was swinging the detector from side to side in front of me as I walked, with the girl pressed so close behind me she kept treading on my heels. Our good fortune held out miraculously. We covered half the ground with no more sound from our handy gadget but a constant, steady hum. Pablo's reconnaissance was paying off. It would seem he'd been right, after all. Then, just as my confidence burgeoned, I heard an ominous click followed by a rapid succession of others. I instantly froze in my tracks, and the girl bumped heavily into my back with a smothered gasp of alarm. I swung the detector round to the right and the clicking intensified. Round to the left, it diminished. When I stepped sideways, it stopped. I actually felt sweat break out on my forehead.

'*Was ist los?*' the girl whispered hoarsely.

'Just stay real close,' I said.

I led them round the hidden killer, but from then on our progress was slow. The clicking hardly stopped at all. There were more live mines on that beach than there'd been on the beaches of Normandy. I was sweating all over now. I could feel it oozing out of my armpits and trickling warm down my ribs, and even the palms of my hands were wet. We zigzagged towards the boom, with the detector rattling like a geiger counter.

Then they drove in the goats.

When the first explosion shattered the night I almost jumped out of my skin. For one split second I thought we had caused it. We were now so close to the boom I could make out a vague white line of surf where the wavelets broke on the shore. I strained every nerve to listen for clicks. A second blast dinned in my ears, and I looked back over my shoulder. Searchlights blazed from the top of every tower, all trained in the same direction – away from us, up the beach. But then the one in the nearest tower began a ranging sweep, and I knew that the Voppos had seen us. The probing finger of light sought us out and pinned us down like moths on a specimen card, and almost at once they opened up.

'Down – and give me the pistol!' I yelled.

She thrust it into my hand, and I pushed myself up on my elbows. It was pretty hopeless, I knew. The range was all of two hundred metres. But I wrapped both hands round the chequered grips and started to blaze away at the cherry-red blossoms of muzzle flash. The staccato yammer of an AKM rattled across the beach. One of them out on the lookout platform. He missed us by several yards, but his raking burst must have hit a mine. It erupted with a roar, showering us with sand and pebbles. Another burst, closer this time, and then the firing suddenly stopped. Probably changing his magazine. I triggered until the Walther was empty, then flung the pistol away and scuttled crabwise out of the glare. I stumbled and fell over Jagersberg, who was lying on top of the girl to shield her body with his own. As I recovered and snatched up the humming detector I couldn't at first understand why the searchlight wasn't

102

tracking me. Then, of course, I knew. Dead-eyed Dick Mackenzie, bless his cotton socks, living up to his ninety-three average over one thousand yards. Somewhere far off, the wail of a siren. More explosions way up the beach. I hauled the professor up on his feet.

'Poor bloody goats,' I said.

'*Bitte?*'

'Oh, nothing. Let's go for a swim.'

Waving my trusty detector I picked our way to the boom at the point where it snaked up out of the sea and joined with the high border fence. The water which lapped around my ankles felt very damned bitterly cold. I had seen that the girl was wearing plimsolls. I kicked off my good black shoes, the only pair I had with me. Fine time to think of that now. I looked at my watch. Nineteen minutes past twelve. Sixty seconds to go. I started a mental count-down.

'Why are we waiting?' Jagersberg whispered.

'Watch the towers,' I said.

Even as I uttered the words, all the lights went out. Pablo's chums had delivered the goods.

'That's it, *now* we can go. We'll pull ourselves out along the boom, then we must swim for the buoy. Me first, then you, Professor. You last,' I said to the girl. 'Are you sure you'll be able to make it?'

'Yes. No trouble at all.'

'Right, then, come on.'

I led them in. The beach shelved quite steeply. Icy water surged round my thighs, and I gasped as it reached my most sensitive parts. I heard the professor gasp, too, and then the bottom dropped away and we were clinging on to the boom.

'You all right, Professor?'

His teeth were chattering hard, but: 'Yes,' he managed, 'I'm fine, Herr Stroud.'

'Good. The jacket will keep you afloat. Pull yourself

along as fast as you can, and when you get tired, just shout.'

The boom was like a long steel scrambling net stretching out into the sea. Very useful. Easier than swimming, and very much faster, too. Especially on the outgoing tide, and in spite of the chilling cold, I felt my spirits rising. But they started to rise too soon. The girl heard it first.

'Herr Stroud – listen!' she called.

I rested on the jacket, numb hands gripping the steel rope mesh, and listened. *Jesus Christ – oh, no!* But yes, the snarl of a big marine engine.

'Keep moving, keep moving!' I yelled.

I started to haul myself through the water, hand over hand down the boom, and realized soon that I had outstripped the old man. As I waited for him to catch up, I took quick stock of the situation, cursing myself all the time for not having thought much earlier that the Voppos might have a boat. We were almost running out of boom but the flashing light on the buoy was still three hundred yards away and the boat was closing quite fast. I could see the upflung spume of its bow-wave cut through the dark rolling sea, and the pinpoints of navigation lights bearing down on us. Then I heard above the engine note the tortured choking gasps of old Professor Jagersberg. As he struggled to pull himself up to me he sounded close to collapse, and I reached out to grab the collar of his jacket. The girl's head bobbed up alongside, and thank God she was still swimming strongly.

'I will help you with him,' she said.

'Yes, but stay by the boom, and be ready to duck!'

I had seen the bow-wave drop. The engine note sank to a whispering burble, and I knew what was coming next. The hard bright beam of the launch's spot sprang suddenly into life, and the swath of white light swung on to the boom not a dozen feet from our heads. At first, it

104

ranged away from us, picking out the mesh like some massive black net curtain. We watched it rove to the beach, then back-track smoothly towards us. I knew that when the time came to duck the jackets would hinder us, So I reached out fast to pull the girl close.

'Get hold of your father's jacket, and when I give you the word, help me pull him under. Do you understand what I mean?'

'Yes,' she said.

'Did you hear that, Professor?'

'Yes. I am ready,' he said.

I reached down as far as I could in the water to take a one-fisted grip on the boom, and fastened my free hand on the collar of his jacket. I could hear him taking deep breaths. The pool of light crept closer and closer . . . ten yards . . . five yards –

'*Now!*'

I gathered my strength and dragged us under. As the beam passed over our heads, the water was lit by a ghostly green glow. Stinging brine clawed at my eyes, but I kept them open until the light died away and all was pitch dark again. I let the jackets lift us then and we surfaced, gasping for air. The girl appeared to be none the worse, but the old man was choking and retching and trying to smother the sound. I tightened my grip on his collar and started to haul away, following the track of the searching spot as it crawled across the swell, reflecting off the whitecaps and lighting up the boom. The girl had not lied when she'd said she could swim. As we towed her father along between us she was easily keeping pace, even though I had the boom to help me.

Now the shaft of light which was ranging the tops of the undulating swell began, it seemed, to recede. I glanced towards its source. It *was* receding. The launch was going slowly astern and suddenly, I realized why. It would be restricted to well-defined channels in the pattern of the mines, and the channels would be much too narrow for comfort. Navigating them, even with the most sophisticated gear, was bound to be a very tricky busines, and the launch could not chase us around by changing course haphazardly. So, once we cleared the end of the boom there was an even chance we'd be home, if not dry.

We made it but, in doing so, came perilously close to the launch. Not much more than thirty yards. I could clearly hear, across the water, urgent clipped commands. Still with the old man clutched between us we struck out for the buoy, on that last but vital three hundred yards. We were trying to swim without too much splash, but Jagersberg was now a dead weight, and it felt as though the swell was rising. We were hampered, too, by our clothes. I felt myself beginning to tire, and the nagging ache in my leg blossomed into stabbing pain as the awful cold bit deeper and deeper to strike at the very bone.

Then the pool of light from the questing spot ranged across the tops of our heads and stopped and began to swing back again. Even as I yelled, the battering din of a heavy machine gun slammed against my ears, and the water around us boiled with shock waves. The burst had come so close I was sure that one of us must be hit, and maybe it was me. I surfaced into blinding light, gulping in lungsful of air, but the jacket stopped me from plunging back under. It was no use, anyway. A loud-hailer crackled.

'You in the water – stay just where you are! Next time, we shall shoot to kill!'

If they did, they couldn't miss. But they couldn't come and get us, either. If they could, they'd be on their way. There had to be a string of mines between us, the very first string in the field. Technically, then, we were out of their territory. Not that they'd give a damn. They'd cut us to pieces, and claim that we'd drifted. The loud-hailer crackled again.

'Swim towards the end of the boom, and then head back to the shore!'

'*Mein Gott!* So close, and they've caught us!'

'Looks like it, love,' I said. 'Better do as they say.'

But as we started to paddle back to the boom, a lot of things happened at once. The glaring light was suddenly extinguished in a splintering of shattered glass and our cold wet world was plunged back into darkness to the sound of a distant shot. Then a second far-off *crack*, and a roar of alarm from the boat. I had actually forgotten Mackenzie. Now, I mentally yelled his name, and kicked about in the water to strike out once more for the buoy. The girl was very quick to catch on. I could feel her helping me, and we instantly began to make headway. A long wild burst from the boat, but this time they were firing blind and the slugs hit yards away. I heard them smack viciously on to the surface, and imagined the upflung spouts.

Apart from the fading rumble of its engine, that was the last we heard from the launch. Then we were swimming wearily in a gently heaving sea, drawing slowly closer to the rolling buoy. Soon, we could hear the water slapping against its sides, and when I made out the dark shape of the *Inga* I could almost have wept with relief. I called out across the water.

'Over here, Fischer – over here!'

He fixed our position with one brief sweep of a hand-lamp, and the *Inga*'s idling engine growled softly as he started to let in the clutch. As the starboard bow drifted past us I lunged with my free left hand and hooked my numbed fingers over the gunwale.

'Cut your engine,' I gasped, 'and get us inboard over the transom.'

The engine died and the little boat rocked as the dark figure up in the cockpit stepped back aft to lean down over the stern.

'You still all right, Professor?' I asked.

'Yes, I'm fine,' he said.

He wasn't fine, he was clearly exhausted, but at least he would revive. We got him under the shallow transom and a pair of hands reached down and between us we managed, without much trouble, to bundle him into the boat. Then:

'Go on, Fräulein,' I said, 'you next.'

I tried to help our rescuer by giving her a boost. He heaved the girl over the transom, then leaned down to give me a hand. A big, hard hand. Thrust viciously, palm downwards, full in the face. I lost my grip on the stern and floundered backwards, half stunned by the blow, eyes filled with tears of pain. My mouth was wide open, and the sea rushed in. When I bobbed up again, windpipe choked with salty mucus, the boat was a yard away and a very good job it was, at that. I felt the churning stream from the prop as the engine burst into life, and back-paddled frantically with flailing arms to stay clear of the whirling bronze blades. As the *Inga* surged off into the night her navigation lights came on, and I watched them draw rapidly away from me. Not towards the moorings at Travemunde, but down-channel, Lübeck-bound. I stared after her lights, my thoughts in a whirl, until they disappeared.

Then, with a belly full of gall, I struck out for the shore.

'What's happening? Where's the boat?'

'Never mind the boat, I'm just about knackered. Give us a hand,' I said.

Mackenzie tugged and I struggled weakly and he dragged me out of the water and I sagged across the pontoon. Then Mackenzie snatched up the gun case, to keep it out of the wet, and squatted down beside me with the case across his knees.

108

'Where's Jagersberg? Was there a change of plan?'

'That's a bloody good question,' I said. 'When I know the answer, I'll tell it to you.'

'But I thought you were well clear. I watched the boat through the night sight until he started to pick you up.'

'You should have watched a bit longer,' I said. 'You'd have seen him give me the push.'

'Give you the push? I don't understand.'

'Neither do I,' I said, 'but I'm bloodywell going to.' I got to my feet. 'Let's get back to the Maritim.'

I took off the sodden life-jacket and left it on the pontoon. The hotel lobby was dimmed and deserted. Mackenzie collected our keys, and the night man watched me drip water on the carpet all the way to the lifts. Perhaps he was used to foreign guests falling into the drink, but in any case he made no comment. We both went up to my room, and I ran a hot bath and talked to Mackenzie as he perched on the lavatory seat.

'We've been double-crossed. The professor's been hijacked.'

'Fischer?'

'I don't know for sure. It was too dark out there to see faces.'

'Who else could it be?' he said.

'Whoever it was hired those yobbos in Hamburg. Somebody who knew the score – hand me that towel, will you? What size of shoe do you take?'

'Shoe? Oh, nine and a half,' he said.

'Better go get me a pair.'

'I've only brown suède.'

'I don't give a monkey's. I can't run around in bare feet.'

'Where are we going, then?'

'The Hundestrasse, in Lübeck.'

'Fischer's house?' he said.

'Maybe. We'll know when we get there.'

'I'll bring some socks as well.'

Lübeck was gloomily deserted. The odd street-light here and there, but the Germans are prudent people and they don't throw money around on unnecessary illumination. We never saw a soul. Hundestrasse was easy to find, but number 40 was not. It was one of five or six renovated cottages, all of them centuries old, which flanked one side of a small cobbled courtyard behind the street's main façade, reached by a narrow arched entrance which ran beneath a three-storey house. The courtyard was lit by one low-powered lamp. The houses were dark and still, and number 40 seemed stillest of all. I tried the thick, studded door, and was seized by a chill premonition as it opened under my hand. Mackenzie pressed in close behind me. I couldn't see a thing, but an ominous smell assailed my nostrils. I heard Mackenzie sniff.

'Find the light-switch, Jock,' I whispered.

'You sure, sir?'

'Yes. Shut the door.'

He closed the door and switched on the light and then we could see where we were. It wasn't so much a hall as a passage which traversed the side of the house. One door facing us, down at the end, and another two on our right. Between these, halfway down the passage, a pair of newel posts suggested a stairway at right-angles to it.

'Bedrooms first,' I said.

The white-painted staircase was steep and narrow. Bird prints climbed the walls. Off the tiny landing, rooms to left and right. No need to check the one on the right. My nostrils led the way. The door was ajar. I pushed it open, and groped on the wall for a switch, and behind me Mackenzie said:

'Oh my God!'

They had tied him down to the bed, and gagged the poor devil to stifle his screams. He must have screamed a lot. The blow-torch they'd used was lying on the floor. It was one of the new-fangled types which are fuelled by a cartridge of liquid gas. There was no skin left on his chest, and the small silver Star of David which hung on a chain round his neck had been welded fast to the scorched black flesh. His eyes were no longer deep-set. They seemed now to bulge half out of his head. The body was still quite warm.

'My God!' Mackenzie said again.

'Cover him up,' I said.

'Who could be so damned inhuman . . .'

'A lot of people, lad. Including some of our lot. Make no mistake about that.'

'Nobody in the Section!'

'Don't you kid yourself, Jock. Anyway, let's take a look around.'

We didn't have the time or the gear to take the house apart, but we made a fairly decent search and the only thing we found was an automatic pistol with one extra magazine. It wasn't really hidden; it was in the drawer of a chest tucked beneath a pile of shirts. Mackenzie unearthed the thing, and handed it across to me. I weighed it in my hand.

'Christ,' I said, 'what's it made of – lead?'

'No, the weight's in the magazine. It's a Heckler & Koch VP-70, fantastic job of design. Eighteen rounds of 9 mm parabellum. It'll fire in bursts of three – but for that you need the shoulder stock. A connection as you lock it in – '

'Never mind the small-arms refresher course, where's the safety?' I said.

'This model doesn't need one. The trigger has a first and second pressure. First pressure cocks the striker, second releases it.'

'I see. That's very interesting. Hand me that spare magazine.'

'You're not thinking of taking it, are you?'

'Right first time,' I said.

'But what about the standing order on the carrying of firearms abroad?'

'Bugger the standing order, we've landed in a very rough league. You've seen what they did to Fischer – well, they're not going to do it to me.'

'The Man isn't going to like it.'

'That's the point,' I said, 'the Man isn't going to *get* it, is he? We're the mugs in the field.'

'I know, but . . .'

'Look, Mackenzie, don't bloody argue! Come on, let's get back to the car.'

We turned off the light as we left the house, and I dropped the latch on the door. The car was still where we'd left it, and I was glad to duck inside. Mackenzie's extremeties were smaller than mine, and his shoes were giving me hell, and when we stopped at a telephone kiosk I got out in my stockinged feet. Harvester sounded wide awake. Perhaps he'd been up all night, waiting for news.

'Yes? Harvester here.'

'Your office at nine o'clock.'

'But what – '

'No, make it half past.'

I put the receiver down. I was far too tired to go into it now. I was badly in need of sleep, and until I'd had at least four hours I was going to be no good at all. Mackenzie had kept the engine running.

'One more call,' I said, 'and then it's off to beddie-byes. Go back via the strand, and stop at the place where the *Inga* was berthed.'

'What happens there?' he said.

'Something which ought to have happened before. We find out the name of the boat on which that mad party was going on.'

112

He climbed smoothly through the gears. 'Why do we want to know its name?'

'Call it a hunch,' I said.

With an extra chair in Harvester's tiny office, there was hardly room to breathe. He listened to my story with an occasional nod of his head, and forebore from interrupting.

'. . . so where was the leak?' I said.

He shrugged his huge bowed shoulders and shook his abundant jowls. 'Your guess, Farrow, is as good as mine.'

'Let's talk about the girl. Why wasn't I told he had a daughter?'

'There was no need for you to know. She and her father were . . . estranged, hadn't seen each other for years. There was never any question – '

'Not much there wasn't!' I said.

'Anyway, you've said she actually helped you.'

'That's beside the point,' I said, 'we're not here to discuss help or hindrance, we're talking about a leak. When was Jagersberg told about the arrangements?'

'Late Friday afternoon.'

'So the girl had a whole day to pass on the message.'

'My dear fellow – who would she tell?'

'How the hell would I know? What have we got on this kid?'

'We don't keep files on everyone, Farrow.'

'Don't give me *that* shit,' I said, 'I'm not asking for a full curriculum vitae.'

The fat man heaved a sigh. 'Well, she used to dance with the E.G. State Theatre – '

'*Used* to dance?' I said. 'What did she do, break an ankle?'

'No, nothing like that,' he said. 'The fact is they . . . er . . . released her.'

113

'So she got the heave, did she?' I said. 'Tell, me, Harvester, why did they sack her?'

'Misbehaviour,' he said.

'What sort of misbehaviour?'

'You know, the usual kind. Conduct unbecoming.'

'You mean she was having it off? Christ, that's what ballet dancers are *for*!'

'Well, that's the story,' he said.

'No, it isn't, Harvester. You're holding something back.' I was rapidly losing my temper. 'Whose bloody side are you *on*?'

'I don't have to take that from you, *mister* Farrow!'

'Don't you? We'll see about that.' I pointed to the telephone. 'Let me speak to the Man.'

'It's Sunday – '

'I know what day it is.'

'All right, calm down,' he said. 'She was shipped back home from London two or three years ago, when the company was appearing at the Opera House. She met some Yank over there, had a whirlwind romance, and was set to defect. But she made the mistake of confiding in a friend who was less of a friend than she'd thought, and – '

'Oh, thanks very much, mate!' I said. 'So why all the bloody secrecy?'

'You're not thinking, are you, Farrow? For the story to have any significance, it would mean that the cousins are to blame for your little spot of bother last night.'

'Christ, you amaze me!' I said. My sarcasm was wasted.

'. . . so it follows, does it not, that the cousins now have old Jagersberg – and didn't you yourself say the cousins would get him in the end?'

'Yes, *in the end*,' I said, 'but the fact remains he was stolen from me, and I bloodywell want him back!'

'Your pride hurt, is it?'

114

'Yes, it is, and I'll tell you something else: you're going to help me get him.'

'You realize, of course,' he said, 'that all of this is pure speculation, that the cousins might not be guilty at all?'

'Sure, but they'll do to start with. By the way, what about those lists I asked you for yesterday morning?'

'I have them here,' he said. He opened the top right-hand drawer of his desk, and came up with two foolscap sheets. 'Names and addresses and all known aliases.'

'Did you get the MOSSAD crowd, too?'

'Yes, both lots are there. But you surely don't think – '

'I don't think anything at all. There's something else you can do for us, though. I want the name of the man who owns a boat called the – what was it, Jock?'

'*Übermensche.*'

'That's right, the *Superman* – got it?' Harvester wrote the name on a pad. 'She's lying up at Travemunde. How soon can you let us know?'

'It's Sunday . . .'

'So you keep telling me.'

'Well, maybe a couple of hours. Where shall I contact you when I've got it?'

'I don't know where we shall be. I'll telephone you here at noon.'

'I'll be at home,' he said, 'but the operator will patch you through.'

I had been glancing down the lists of names. None of the first lot meant anything to me, but one of the names on the list of cousins immediately caught my eye. It had been scrawled on the bottom, in pencil, as though as an afterthought.

'I see you've added Francis Toomey to the Company list,' I said. 'Why was that?'

'He's a late arrival.'

'When did he get here?' I said.

'Yesterday morning.'

115

'Up from Madrid?'

Harvester's bushy eyebrows climbed his high domed head. 'Yes, that's right. Do you know him?'

'Just a passing acquaintance,' I said. My solitary meeting with Toomey, near Burgos, had not been an amiable one. 'Have we any idea what brings him to Hamburg?'

'No we haven't,' Harvester said.

'Where's he staying?'

'We think at the US Consulate-General.'

'What's his cover there?'

'He has a roving commission with the trade delegation.'

'Interesting,' I said. 'Well, come on, Mackenzie, we'd better be on our way.'

'Where are you going?' Harvester asked quickly. 'What d'you intend to do?'

'When I decide, I'll let you know.'

'Now look here, Farrow – ' he said.

'Yes?' I said.

'We're supposed to liaise . . .'

'We *are* liaising,' I said. 'What more do you want?'

He looked slightly flustered. 'What about our car?'

'We haven't finished with it yet.'

'It's registered here, you know, and we don't want any comeback.'

'You should have thought about that,' I said, 'when you started messing about with doubles.'

'I'm warning you, Farrow,' he said, 'that I intend to encode a report right away.'

'Yes, you do that,' I said.

Outside, the copper-green spire of St Peter's was slickly wet with the rain which now fell in driving needles out of a cloudy but ice-blue sky. We were parked in a nearby waiting zone, empty spaces all over the place and the meters, on Sunday, not in use. Mackenzie slid quickly under the wheel and leaned across the car to unlatch my door. As we started the engine:

116

'Where are we going?' he said.

'Remember that little café, just off the Mittelweg?'

'The one with the pickled herrings?'

'Yes. Could you find it again?'

'I think so.'

'Right, let's go, then.'

I wouldn't say he took the most direct route, but he eventually got us there, and was able to park within yards of the entrance. As he locked up the car, I hurried down the worn stone steps to get in out of the damp. It was early for a Sunday morning, only quarter past ten, and the place had no other customers. I sat at a table down at the end, the one I had chosen before, and was joined by Mackenzie almost at once. The buxom girl was not yet on duty. The barman served us himself, and then went back to rattling his bottles.

'Well, Mackenzie,' I said, 'what d'you make of our overweight colleague now?' He answered me with a stare of prudent expectation. 'Come on, lad,' I went on, 'I'm waiting to hear what you think of the bugger.'

He finger-combed his blond hair, and took an exploratory sip of his coffee. Then: 'I was rather intrigued,' he said, 'as to how he was able to take it so calmly.'

'But that's Harvester's forte,' I said. 'He has his reputation to think of. Anyway, do go on.'

'And when we turned up without the professor, he not only wasn't alarmed, he didn't even seem unduly surprised.'

'You mean you think he *knew*?'

'Good Lord, no!' he said hastily. 'I wouldn't suggest such a thing!'

'Wouldn't you? I would.'

'You can't be serious!'

'Just keep your voice down,' I said, 'and listen while I tell you a story.' He watched me pack a pipe, a worried frown on his smooth young face. A pity to disillusion him, but he might as well learn now, before someone dropped him in it. 'SIS have a plan to get Jagersberg out, but the cousins want him, as well, and their need for him is greater than ours. So, our lot do a deal. They send in a low-grade expendable – it's that sort of dicey job – and if he doesn't make it, too bad, because the boffin gets taken out, too, and at least the Others are robbed of his know-how. If, on the other hand, Herbie Stroud manages to work the oracle, the plot moves into phase two. The cousins are told the where, and the when, and – '

'Excuse me,' Mackenzie broke in, 'but *why* a phase two? Why not just hand him over?'

'I'll tell you why,' I said, 'because this thing's bigger than just the Section. I doubt if the Man would agree to risking the loss of one of his own for the sake of the CIA. I think he'd tell the bastards to stuff it.'

I was using young Mackenzie as Charlie had often used me, as a sort of handy sounding board.

'Yes, I'm with you there,' he said, 'but what about that business with Fischer? If we accept your phase two, why should anyone want to work him over?'

'Ah, now that,' I said, 'is where the *triple*-cross comes in. Unless I miss my guess, Fischer was doubling for MOSSAD. The Israelis want Jagersberg, too.'

'It would figure. They're known to be working on lasers.'

'They're working on everything.'

'Even so, it doesn't explain – '

'Patience, son,' I said. 'Let's assume that the cousins had staked out Fischer's house, and were waiting to relieve him of Jagersberg when he took the old man home. But Fischer has already handed the Jagersbergs over to his MOSSAD buddies, and goes on to his house alone . . .'

'The cousins make him tell them where the Jagersbergs have gone.'

'No, not necessarily. For a start, he might not have known, and even if he did – '

'God! He must have told them!'

'No. They were in a hurry, you see. They might have gone too far too fast.'

'It's possible, I suppose.'

'You'd better hope it's more than possible. If the cousins have Jagersberg, it'll be a damn' sight harder to get him back.'

'Pretty hopeless, I'd say. He's probably on his way to the States right now.'

'Don't be negative, Jock. Try to look on the bright side.'

'If the Israelis have him, what then?'

'They could have a problem getting him out, especially if he doesn't want to go. And don't forget there's the girl, as well.'

'So where do you think they might be?'

'Stashed away in a MOSSAD safe house.'

'In Hamburg?'

'Probably. It's most unlikely they'd keep him in Lübeck.'

'So all we have to do is find one house in a very large city.'

'You've hit the nail on the head. Listen – you want some herrings?'

'Er, no, I don't think so,' he said. 'Not at half past ten in the morning.'

'Fair enough, I suppose. What about another coffee, then?'

'That's different. Yes, please,' he said. The barman brought us two fresh cups, and when he had moved away, Mackenzie leaned across the table. 'I'm still a bit puzzled, you know, over your little shindig on Friday evening.'

'A not-unusual Company balls-up, typical CIA. The

local Chief of Station acting on his own. He knows their mob's after Jagersberg, but he hasn't been told the full score. Then he gets the buzz that we've flown into town and he knows, or suspects, why we've come. So he puts in some heavies to slow me down.'

'You mean he wasn't aware we were slated to do the job *for* them?'

'It wouldn't surprise me at all. That lot's so bloody clever-clever it simply isn't true.'

'But somebody must have been fully briefed.'

'Most likely Toomey,' I said, 'and probably because he knows me by sight. Don't forget he didn't arrive here until the morning after my scrap.'

'It all seems so unbelievable!'

'Christ, don't be naive, lad,' I said. 'You might as well say you still can't imagine Harvester being in the know.'

'To tell you the truth, I'm finding it hard. He's a Section man, after all.'

'He's a Section man who's been put out to grass. Most of his present-day work is with our own Central Intelligence wallahs.'

'Yes, but even so . . .'

'Anyway, I don't give a chuff, it's academic now. But from this point on, we don't trust the bugger.'

'What if we need his assistance?'

'That's another matter. If MOSSAD does have our man, he's going to help us to get him back. So we'll ask for whatever we need, but we'll tell him nothing – you got that?'

'Anything you say.' He watched me drain the dregs of my coffee. 'But where do we begin?'

'We begin by finding out for certain who's got Jagersberg, and I'll tell you how we're going to do it – how's your *plattdeutsch*, by the way?'

'You want me to pose as a native of Hamburg?'

'Only on the phone.'

120

'Yes, I think I could manage the dialect.'

'Good, then here's what you're going to do. You're going to ring the US Consulate and say you want to speak to one of their *profis* about a certain missing person – no, better say missing old man. Say you'll call again at 1130. That'll give them a chance to pass your message to the proper quarter. Then when you ring a second time we'll see who comes on the phone. If it's Toomey, I think I might recognize his voice just as he might recognize mine.'

'I see. What do I say to him?'

'It's best if you improvise, but don't mention Jagersberg by name. Just say you know where he is, and that you're willing to shop him for ten thousand marks.'

'Isn't that rather high?'

'If you sell it too cheap, he'll smell a rat. He'll be leery, anyway, but if they don't have Jagersberg, he won't dare to pass up the chance that you really know what you're talking about. Tell him to take the cash to the Rabenstrasse passenger-launch jetty and get on board the first boat which leaves the pier after twelve o'clock.'

'What if he doesn't agree?'

'If you're turned down out of hand, it'll almost certainly mean that they've got Jagersberg already.'

'And it'll put them on their guard.'

'We'll just have to risk that.'

'Right, where's the phone?'

'We'll phone from the Schloss Hotel, from one of the lobby kiosks.'

'Shall we walk down or take the car?'

'The car. Your shoes are killing me.'

'I say, I *am* sorry,' he said.

The phone booth reminded me of Harvester's office. With the pair of us crammed inside, it was just about as claustrophobic, and Mackenzie's brown suède shoes felt even tighter than before. Mackenzie held the phone, and we leaned our heads together so that I could hear what was being said. His Hamburg accent sounded for real, and he carried it off very well. This was our second call to the consulate, and the voice which was coming over the wire to us this time might have been that of Francis Toomey. It was the same mid-western drawl, but it had been a long time and he was speaking in German and I simply couldn't be sure.

'. . . you'd better tell me who you are.'

'No names,' Mackenzie said. 'Are you, or are you not, interested?'

'Hold on – ' the voice said again. Whoever was at the other end of the line did not speak German well, and was obviously struggling with the *plattdeutsch* gutturals.

'Look,' Mackenzie said, 'make up your mind, or I phone the *Russkis*.'

'No, wait – '

'I will wait just ten more seconds . . . well, do we have a deal?'

'All right, but I'm going to need guarantees.'

'You will get them on the boat. Come alone, and don't forget the money.'

'Now listen, any tricks . . .'

'No tricks, just bring the ten thousand.'

I nodded, and he put the receiver down, and we stepped out into the lobby to breathe some unused air.

'How did I do?'

'Just fine,' I said.

'Hadn't we better get down to the pier?'

'It's only a two-minute trip. Let's check in, and then I'll phone the fat man.'

'Do you think that boat might be a lead?'

'Not now, not really,' I said, 'but we might as well have the information for future reference. Could you fetch our stuff from the car?'

'Yes, of course,' he said. 'What about the Husqvarna?'

'Leave that where it is. We can think about ditching it later. Right now, it's safer locked in the boot.'

At that very early stage in the season we had no problem getting two rooms, and Mackenzie went off to bring up our luggage. As soon as he was away, I contacted Percy Harvester. He was waiting for my call, and ready for the information. He told me that the owner of the *Übermensche* was one Kurt Wintzer, senior partner in a firm of office-equipment suppliers. Wintzer lived out north-west of the airport at a place called Langenhorn.

'Any known connections?'

Absolutely none. You're barking up the wrong tree, Farrow.'

'Perhaps. We'll see,' I said. 'Anyway, there's something else you can do.'

'What is it this time?' he said.

'Find out the names and locations of every Israeli ship currently berthed in Hamburg.'

'That sounds more like it,' he said.

'Also those expected to dock within the next few days.'

'You're sure they have him, then?'

I was pretty sure that *he* was sure, but: 'No, I'm not,' I said, 'I'm merely covering all contingencies.'

'Very wise. By the way, I've been in touch with home control.'

'I thought you might have,' I said, 'so what's the good word?'

'Instructions are, you're to give it two more days. Or, to be exact, until Tuesday morning.'

'If we haven't got our man back by then, we might as well go home in any case.'

'That's the general idea. Now – is there anything else you require?'

'Not at the moment, no.'

'Right. Keep in touch.'

'You betcha.'

'What?'

'Nothing, I just sneezed,' I said.

Mackenzie drove us down to the Alsterufer, and we parked illegally just short of the junction with Rabenstrasse.

'You stay with the car, Jock,' I said. 'I'll nip down and see if he's already there.'

'Suppose it's not Toomey?' he said.

'No sweat, I can spot a cousin a mile off.'

As though my getting out of the car was a signal, it immediately began to rain, and I mourned for my abandoned raincoat. Without it, I felt conspicuous on such a lousy day. Bad enough to be wearing my Burton's blue serge with a pair of brown suède shoes. As I hurried through the small park towards the dinghy marina which fronted the landing stage, I drew curious stares from a Darby and Joan who were walking a little dog. The old dear was wearing a yellow plastic rainhood. I nodded as I passed.

The rainswept pier was deserted. All those waiting for the boat were milling around in the café. I entered the damp, steamy fug and eased through the throng of coffee-drinking tourists to a picture-postcard stand. It was one of those tall revolving jobs, almost as tall as me, and it made a pretty good vantage point from which to check the place. It did not take me long to determine that Toomey wasn't yet there. Nor was anyone else, I decided, remotely like a Company man. Most of the sightseers were couples, and most were elderly. I skulked behind my postcard rack and patiently bided my time, watching the tall wide windows which looked out on to the lake.

At twelve o'clock there was still no sign of a possible Company man, and five minutes later the boat hove in sight. All but a few of the café's patrons began to troop outside. The long white boat nudged up to the dock, and some passengers disembarked, and still no sign of Toomey. I moved away from my postcard rack and crossed to the magazine stand, and peered through the rain-spotted window over on the landward side. Toomey hadn't changed a bit. I knew him right away. He was running down the path which flanked the marina, and soon he was out of sight behind the side of the café. Back to my postcard rack. I watched him join the straggle of people queueing to get on the boat, and saw him step across her gangplank. He was the last to board. A deck-hand replaced the hand-rail, and she began to slide away. I was about to do the same when I saw Toomey suddenly turn round, as though he'd heard somebody call his name. Then, I saw that somebody *had*.

The caller was young, in his middle twenties. He was wearing a light-coloured mac, and a soft grey hat with a very narrow brim. He sprinted along the pier, waving a small yellow envelope of the kind in which telegrams come. Toomey leaped to the rail and shouted something. I couldn't hear what he said, but he swept his right arm round in an arc and pointed across the lake towards the jetty at Uhlenhorster Färhaus. The signal was obvious, and clear. He was telling the lad to drive round the lake and meet him on the other side. The boat was now forty yards offshore, and no way would it turn back, so Toomey was stuck for a good twenty minutes. The young man nodded emphatically to show that he'd understood, and stuffed the envelope back in his pocket. Then he turned on his heel to head back towards the Alsterufer. I took off after him, and I didn't much care if Toomey saw me. There wasn't a damn thing he could do.

I caught up with the messenger boy as he hurried through the park, and he heard my rapid footsteps behind him. As he turned his head, I dragged the pistol out of my waistband and rammed it hard into his side.

'Just slow down a bit, sonny, and let's walk nicely,' I said, 'and keep your hands in your pockets. You see that dark blue sedan?'

'Y . . . yes.'

'Well, that's where we're heading.'

'Jesus, what is this?' he said.

'I'll tell you when we get there. If you want to live to eat lunch, keep your mouth shut and do as you're told.'

Thank God for a rainy Sunday morning. There were very few people about, and those who were paid no heed to us. As we approached the car, Mackenzie hopped out and moved round the bonnet. He looked only slightly surprised.

'Anything I can do to help?'

'Yes, open the back door,' I said, 'and let's have him in, before he gets wet.' I shouldered in at his side, and felt him all over for hard things. 'Well, now, what have we here?' I thrust my free hand inside his raincoat and under his jacket, too. He was wearing a spring-type shoulder rig. I jerked the pistol free, and passed it across to Mackenzie, who was now in the driver's seat.

'Smith & Wesson .375.'

'Very naughty,' I said. 'Since when have you people been allowed to tote these things around in the sovereign state of West Germany?'

'Who the hell are you?' he said.

'Why, we're your loyal allies. I thought you'd have realized that.'

'Listen, if you guys are limeys – '

'Watch your language, m'boy. You're looking at a real Scottish laird. Now – let's have that envelope, eh?'

'No dice! That's classified informa . . . aaarggh!'

I hit him across the side of one cheek with the barrel of the H & K. Not very hard, just hard enough. His head snapped back and his hat toppled off and his hands

126

flew up to his face, and I pulled the envelope out of his pocket.

'Watch him, Jock,' I said.

Mackenzie cocked the Smith & Wesson. I tore at the envelope's flap, and unfolded the small slip of paper it held. The message, very brief, was timed at 1151.

The girl is loose, it said, *and has phoned from Wedel S-bahn station. Have told her to stay right there. Await instructions. FCG.*

'Have you any idea, Mackenzie,' I said, 'how far Wedel is from here?'

'I'd say about fifteen or sixteen miles.'

'Which is the fastest, train or car?'

'I'd go for the train, every time.'

'Even in Sunday traffic?'

'Definitely,' he said. 'I believe there's a very good service.'

'Drive to the Hauptbahnof, then, and don't spare the horses. We're in a hurry.'

The unfortunate young cousin made it easy for me by bending his head almost down to his knees to hold his face in both hands. The carotid area was nicely exposed. I switched the pistol from right fist to left and chopped with the edge of my hand, and as he pitched forward between the seats I grabbed at the scruff of his neck and dragged him sideways and pushed him down in a crumpled heap on the floor. Then I tucked the pistol back into my waistband, and leaned forward over the squab. Mackenzie was driving very fast. We had crossed the Kennedybrücke and were turning sharp right on to Glockengiesser-wall, with the station way up on our left. There was hardly any traffic about.

'Listen, Jock,' I said, 'when you've dropped me off, drive on out of town. It doesn't matter where. This joker should sleep for a good fifteen minutes. When he starts to come round, ditch him and move yourself back to the Schloss. I'll get in touch with you there.'

As he drew up at the railway station, he twisted round in his seat. 'What shall I do with the Smith & Wesson?'

'Spoils of war,' I said. 'Keep it, it might come in handy.'

He did not waste any time. He let in the clutch as I slammed the door. I watched the car roar away, then turned and ran down the station concourse. A railway uniform. I grabbed the man's arm.

'Which platform for Wedel?'

He pointed, 'Right at the end.'

As I dashed across the walkway which spanned the platforms I could hear a train rumbling in, and I didn't bother with the ticket machine. I clattered down the steps, brushing rudely past those climbing up, and jumped aboard the train just before the doors hissed shut.

A stylized chart above the windows showed Wedel at the end of the line, with a dozen stations in between. Nothing to do but relax. I filled a pipe. A woman leaned forward to tap me on the knee, and point to a sign which said *Rauchen Verboten*. I put the pipe away, and the woman smiled, and nodded. I smiled and nodded back. Dammtor, then Sternschanze, then Holstenstrasse . . . and so on down the line. I worried at every successive station in case an inspector got on, but as we pulled out of Rissen I knew that this was my lucky day. We rolled into Wedel a few minutes later.

I found her in one of the open-faced shelters, huddled on the slatted seat. She was wearing a skirt and sweater, no coat. Her tousled hair looked wet, and she was hugging herself against the cold. I saw her before she saw me.

'*Guten Tag, Fräulein Jagersberg.*'

She looked up and recognized me, and her eyes opened wide with shock and alarm. 'Why, Herr Stroud!' she said. 'But I telephoned – '

128

'Yes, I know all about it.'

'But what are *you* doing here?'

'I've come to take you somewhere safe.'

'I'm so confused . . .' she said. She seemed to be on the verge of tears.

'Now don't you worry,' I said. 'Everything's going to be all right.'

'No . . . you don't understand.'

'Oh, I think I do. Come on, let's find the ticket machine.'

The train had pulled slowly out of the station but now it came trundling back, having switched at the points to the up-line. I sought out a corner seat in a carriage which was virtually empty, and the girl let me usher her in. She seemed crushed and defeated, utterly worn out.

'I want you to tell me,' I said, 'exactly what has happened to you since we parted company last night.'

She leaned against me, shivering, and spoke in such a low voice I had difficulty hearing her over the rumbling of the train. It was very largely as I'd surmised. After abandoning me, the boat had run on down to Lübeck, and they'd transferred there to a car.

'How many people were waiting for you?'

'A man, and a woman,' she said.

'Those her clothes you're wearing?'

'I think so.'

'Where did you go from there? Did the man from the boat go with you?'

'No, the man from the boat went away, and I don't know where the others took us. It was dark, and my father was ill, and . . .'

'All right, we'll come back to that later. Who did you think they were?'

'I . . . I . . .'

'You thought they were Americans, didn't you?'

'No!'

'Don't lie to me, Fräulein,' I said. 'I'm here to help you – remember?'

'Where are you taking me now?'

'That depends upon whether you tell me the truth.'

She chewed at her lower lip, then sniffed and nodded miserably. 'All right, yes, there was an arrangement.'

'Damned right there was,' I said, 'and it didn't include me!'

She shook her head quickly and put a small hand on my arm. 'They promised me nobody would be harmed – you must believe that!' she said.

'Very well, I believe you. Who were "they"?'

'The Americans, I suppose. I never actually saw them.'

'How did they first contact you?'

'It started with a telephone call.'

'And after that?' I said.

'Messages from my . . .'

'Boy friend in London?'

'Yes, from Robert,' she said.

'How were the messages delivered?'

As if I didn't know. They had used a series of dead-letter drops, never the same one twice, their locations being passed at specific times via a public telephone box. A simple but effective system employed by one and all. What did intrigue me, though, was the fact that the Company must have been plotting for such a very long time without taking any real action. But I had to stop questioning the girl because when we reached Bahrenfeld station, four teenagers boarded the train and chose to seat themselves opposite us. Our silence then gave me time to develop an idea at the back of my mind, sparked off as I checked the train's progress by the chart on the carriage wall. The chart was laid out exactly like those on the London Underground, with the interchange stations clearly marked. The Wedel track, coloured green, was crossed at Sternschanze by one of bright yellow. This was

130

a U-bahn line, and the second stop down was St Pauli. Suddenly, I made up my mind, and as we drew out of Holstenstrasse:

'Ours is the next stop,' I said.

The girl just nodded with dumb resignation. We switched to the underground train and rode it down to St Pauli, at the end of the Reeperbahn. When we hit the street it was no longer raining and the bracing, washed-clean air seemed crisper and colder. The girl's teeth were chattering. I took her by the arm, and we crossed the wide dual carriageway. I knew where I wanted to go, but I wasn't quite sure how to get there. Halfway up Cuxhaven Allee I recognized the turn, and soon we were at the apartment block. The girl looked up at the building.

'What is this place?' she said.

I think she knew instinctively. She tried to tug away, but I held her arm and shook her gently.

'Now just you listen to me! You don't have any papers, I can't take you to an hotel –'

'I know, but why *here*?'

'Because it's safe – and there's nowhere else to go.'

She wasn't happy about it, but she let me nudge her inside and tramped up the stairs ahead of me. When we reached the carpeted landing, I put my hands on her shoulders and positioned her beside the door. Then I knocked, and someone within called:

'Who is it?'

'It's me,' I said, 'from Friday night – remember?'

'Just a moment . . .'

She opened the door, and then stood back and opened her arms. She was wearing the same négligee, and the same wide smile of welcome.

'Darling – come in!' she said, 'I didn't expect to see *you* again! Here, let me look at your eye . . .'

'Wait,' I said, 'I've got someone with me.'

She poked her blonde head round the door, and when

131

she saw the girl she chuckled and punched me on the arm. 'Ah, so! You want a little threesome!'

'No, it's nothing like that,' I said, 'you don't understand – look, can we come in?'

She hesitated, and sighed, then '*Schatz*, why not?' she said. She led on through her perfumed chamber into a cosy sitting room which was probably out of bounds to clients. The room was small, but richly furnished. The wages of sin are tax-free. Satin-covered sofa and chairs, stereo, neat little bar, a carved Venetian mirror, and a couple of handsome lamps. Our hostess squeezed behind the bar counter. 'Well, don't just stand there,' she said, 'both of you find a seat somewhere. Would you like a drink?'

The girl remained standing, lost and frightened. 'Thank you, no,' she said.

'Yes, please,' I said. 'Have you got any whisky?'

'I've got everything, darling,' she said. 'Do you take it with ice?'

'No, thanks, just water.'

'In the bathroom,' she said.

She handed me a well-charged glass, and as I left the room I realized that the girl must be thinking I knew my way around. So what the hell, what did it matter. Let her think what she liked. When I got back to the sitting room she was crouched on a leather pouffe, mute and silent.

'Cheers,' I said. 'Look – I don't know your name.'

'You can call me Suzi,' she said. She settled herself into one of the armchairs. 'Now, what's this all about?' I perched on an arm of the sofa. 'Don't sit there,' she went on, 'sit properly, and tell me what you want.'

'Yes, well, the fact is,' I said, 'it's about the girl – '

'You surprise me!'

' – she needs a place to stay, and I thought . . .'

'You thought she might stay here? But that's impossible!' she said, 'I have my work.'

'I know, but couldn't you take a couple of days off?'

'Soon I shall have to,' she said, 'but in the meantime . . .'

'I'd pay, of course.'

'How *much* would you pay?' she said. She sipped at her drink.

'How much do you want?'

'Listen to me,' the girl said, 'I do not wish to stay here!'

'Please be quiet. How much?' I said again.

Suzi eyed me shrewdly. 'For two whole days and nights?'

I did a swift calculation. 'Eight hundred marks,' I said.

'Make it twelve hundred and fifty.'

'No, make it a thousand,' I said.

'Done – provided you promise no trouble.'

'That's the last thing we need,' I said. I kicked off my borrowed footwear, and massaged my tortured toes. Suzi gestured with her glass.

'What is wrong with your feet?'

'I'm wearing somebody else's shoes.'

'Why not buy some of your own?'

'Because,' I said, 'it's Sunday, and all the shops are closed.'

She laughed. 'No, they're not, not all of them. There are shops not far from here which are open seven days a week. I'll show you where they are, if you like, as I shan't be working today!'

But that would mean leaving the girl, and I couldn't take the risk of her running away, so, 'Listen, Suzi,' I said, 'would you like to nip out and buy a pair for me?'

'You will need to try them on!'

'No, I won't. You can take these brown shoes with you and tell them you want a pair a full size bigger, with a wider fitting. Plain black, not too dear.'

'Suppose when I bring them you don't like the style?'

'I have faith in your taste,' I said.

I think she realized I wanted her out of the way, so I could talk to the girl, and I sensed that she was enjoying the intrigue. 'All right, then,' she said, 'I'll go as soon as I put on some clothes.'

She rose, and left the room, and I crouched on the carpet in front of the girl. 'Now, tell me what happened,' I said, 'when you got to the house. Tell me how you escaped.'

She heaved a drawn-out, shuddering sigh. 'I'm tired, and my head aches,' she said.

'I know, but this is important,' I urged, 'try to remember – please.'

She spoke in a low, dispirited mumble. By the time they got down to Lübeck, the old man had been so weak the two men had needed to carry him off the boat and into the car.

'. . . there were blankets. We wrapped them around us, but my father could not get warm. Long before we reached the house he was worse, he was shivering all the time. They had to carry him down all those steps . . .'

'Down what steps?' I said.

'The house was on the side of a hill, some distance from the road. First, there was a footpath, but it soon became so steep that it turned into a long flight of steps. The house has a roof of straw, and a tiny garden with a monkey tree in it.'

'How could you see, in the dark?'

'I saw it this morning, when I – '

'Of course. Sorry, go on,' I said.

'The man undressed my father, and put him into bed.'

'Upstairs or down?'

'In an upstairs room. The woman made hot drinks, and I think she must have put something into mine because the next thing I knew it was morning. I was lying, undressed, in a bed, and these clothes' – she plucked at her sweater – 'were laid out over a chair.'

'So you put them on, and then what?'

'I went to see my papa. He was running a very high temperature. The man was worried,' she said.

'Can you describe these people to me?'

'The man was dark, and tall . . .'

'As tall as me?'

'No.'

'How much shorter?'

'Ten centimetres,' she said. 'Also, he was not so heavy. His eyes were black, or dark brown, and I think he would be about forty years old.'

'That's good. Now, the woman,' I said. 'No – wait a moment.'

Suzi barged in. She was all dressed up for the street but not, I could see, in her working clothes. She was wearing a green boucle suit, and the sort of smart cape they sell at Jaeger's. Her shoes looked expensive, too, and the overall effect was impressive. The little dog pranced around her feet on the end of a thin, plaited lead, and she was carrying a snazzy shopping bag. I passed her the brown suède shoes, and gave her a couple of fifty-mark notes. Another twenty-five quid.

'Will that be enough?'

'I think so. I'll be back in about an hour.'

'All right if I use your telephone – local call?' I said.

'Local Hamburg, or local New York?'

'Hamburg, I promise,' I said.

'Help yourself, in that case. What about your little friend?'

'What about her?'

'She needs a coat.'

'We'll think of that later,' I said.

She shrugged. 'If anyone should call, tell them I'm engaged.'

'Right, I'll do that.'

When she was gone, I turned again to the girl. 'You were telling me about the woman. How old would you say she would be?'

'As old as the man, about forty.'

'Much the same build as yourself?'

'Perhaps a size larger. She had straight black hair, just turning grey, high cheekbones, and a rather wide mouth.'

'Anything else? Any other distinguishing features?'

She frowned. 'I don't think so,' she said.

'All right. So why did you run away?'

'It was in the morning,' she said, 'I heard them talking at my father's bedside. They were concerned about him, you see.'

'What were they saying?'

'I don't know. They were speaking in a language which sounded strange to me. It was then I realized that something was wrong. I asked them who they were, but they wouldn't tell me. They said not to worry, that soon we would leave that place and go where we'd both be safe for ever.'

'They didn't tell you where?'

'No. I don't think they cared about me. It was Father – '

'Yes, I know.'

'Do you also know who these people were?'

'I certainly do,' I said. 'They were – *are* – working for Israel.'

'No!'

'You'd better believe it,' I said. 'They stole a march on your Yankee friends, just like you stole a march on me. Anyway, go on with your story.'

She put a hand to her head. 'Could I have some aspirin, please?'

'Yes, of course,' I said. 'Are you hungry? Do you want something to eat?'

136

'No, they gave me breakfast,' she said.

'But it's lunch-time now – '

'Please – just the aspirin.'

'Wait here, I'll find some,' I said.

Suzi had a large bathroom cabinet stocked with proprietary drugs, some with international brand-names. Including Mogadon. Which looks much the same as aspirin. I shook two into my hand, and rinsed out a tooth-glass and filled it with water. As the girl swallowed the pills, I felt a little twinge of conscience.

'Thank you, Herr Stroud,' she said.

'Now then, how did you manage to get away?'

'It was quite easy, really,' she said. 'Soon after they'd talked at my father's bedside, the man put on his coat. I think he was going to get medicines. When I went back upstairs to sit with my father, I saw a key in the bedroom door. I waited several minutes, and then I called downstairs to tell the woman my father was worse. She came up to see for herself, and I locked her in and ran out of the house.'

'Leaving your father,' I said.

She looked up quickly. 'I'm no fool, Herr Stroud. I know his value to them. They would not harm a hair of his head.'

'So what did you hope to achieve?'

'My only thought was to get away. I ran up the hill, into town, looking for a telephone box. I couldn't find one at first, and then I saw the S-bahn station and I knew there would be one there. Then as I ran into the station, I heard a train coming in, and I didn't stop to think. I just jumped on. I stayed on to the end of the line, at that place – '

'Wedel.'

'Yes, that's right. I telephoned from there.'

'You phoned the US Consulate.'

'Yes. I had no money, of course. I had to reverse the charges.'

'Who did you speak to?' I said.

'A man. He didn't tell me his name. He just said – '

'I know the rest.'

'*How* did you know?'

'That's not important. Now, listen carefully. If you don't, you might never see your father again.'

'No! Don't say that!' she said.

'I'm saying it, Fräulein. It's all up to you.'

'I want Robert . . .'

'I can't promise that. I can't really promise anything, except that I mean to try and get your father away from these people.'

'What happens then?' she said.

'I'm taking you both back to England.'

'But I want – '

'I know what you want,' I said, 'you want to go to America. Well, you probably will, in time, but *only* of you behave yourself. Do I make myself perfectly clear?'

She nodded. 'Yes. I will do as you say.'

'You must stay here until I come to fetch you. Don't stick your nose outside, and if Suzi questions you, tell her nothing. *Nothing* – you understand?'

'Yes, I understand.' She looked pale and drawn, dark rings round her eyes. 'I feel exhausted,' she said.

The Mogadon.

'Suzi will put you to bed, but first you must promise to do nothing foolish.'

'I trust you, Herr Stroud,' she said.

'That's good. Come on, lie down on the sofa.' I helped her up off the pouffe, and settled her on the satin cushions. 'There, that's better,' I said, 'just relax.'

She closed her eyes and I went across to the bar and helped myself to another stiff Scotch. Then, I used the phone.

'Mackenzie?'

'God! I've been worried!'

'Worry no more,' I said. 'Bring the car down to Ludwigstrasse, number fifty-three.' I told him how to get there. '. . . you got that?'

'Yes, I'll find it,' he said. 'What's happening?'

'How much cash have you got?'

'Around about four hundred marks.'

'Bring it with you,' I said. 'Did you have any trouble with the cousin?'

'None to speak of,' he said. 'I dropped him off in Borgfelde.'

'Make sure you're not followed,' I said.

'I will. I'll be there in fifteen minutes.'

'Listen, Mackenzie,' I said, 'the main thing is to be *sure* you're not tailed!'

'I heard you the first time,' he said.

Well, you've got to trust somebody sometime, and the lad was proving his worth. I went back into the sitting room. The girl was fast asleep. Suddenly, I felt very hungry. I sat down to finish my drink, but was only halfway through it when I heard the front door bang. Suzi bustled in, beaming.

'Try those for size,' she said.

She handed me a rectangular parcel. I tore the wrappings off and opened the box and looked at the shoes.

'Oh, very nice,' I said. They were, too, and, what's more, they fitted. As I put them on, Suzi packed Mackenzie's hand-lasted suèdes into the empty box.

'Are they really comfortable?'

'Absolutely,' I said.

'Now, what shall we do with the little one?'

'Nothing, just let her rest.'

Suzi slipped off her cape. 'Lift her into a chair, and I'll make up the sofa,' she said. She went off, and came back with her arms full of blankets. 'Perhaps she might like a bath?'

'No, let her sleep. She can have a bath later.'

Suzi made up a sofa-bed, then very gently, with much soft coaxing, she helped the girl undress. It seemed that long-dormant maternal instincts were stirring in her ample breast. She tossed a thin slip on the back of the chair.

'A summer slip!' she said. 'It'll be a miracle if this poor child doesn't catch her death of cold!'

As I glanced down at the flimsy garment, something caught my eye. A row of tiny black-inked symbols. The ubiquitous laundry mark. I took careful note of the letters and numerals.

'What are you doing?' Suzi said.

'Nothing. Listen, Suzi, tell he something,' I said, 'what's the name of that little place on the hill – you know, the one with no streets . . .'

'Blankanese?'

'Yes, I think that's the one.'

'It is very *schön*,' she said. 'You can get there by passenger boat, if you want to, but then it's a slog up the hill. Are you thinking of paying a visit? You will find many shops open there, as it's quite a tourist attraction. Lots of people go. The houses are old, and very quaint – '

'So I understand. Well, you seem to have made her comfortable.'

She looked down at the sleeping girl. 'She's so young, and so pretty – who is she?'

'No questions. That's part of our deal.'

She smiled. 'I'm sorry. All right, no questions. But talking about our deal . . .'

'Five hundred now, and five hundred later. I haven't got it yet, but I will have as soon as my friend arrives.'

'Good. Would you like some lunch? I can give you cold chicken – '

'That's kind,' I said, 'but I need to be on my way.'

I moved across to the window and looked down into the street, taking an occasional sip at the Scotch, watching for the car. A few minutes later, it rounded the corner and drew up in front of the house. Suzi was busy in her tiny kitchen. I could hear her moving around, and the slam of a fridge door opening and closing. Mackenzie hopped out of the car, and looked up at the front of the building. He saw me at the window, and waved, and I motioned him to come on up. Suzi let him in, and looked him over with an appraising eye.

'Are we going to be introduced?'

'No. And your chicken's getting cold.' She shook a mock fist at me, and went back into the kitchen. 'In here, Jock,' I said.

I led him into the sitting room, and he looked at the girl on the couch. 'Is this – '

I held up a warning hand. 'Yes, it is,' I said. 'Did you bring the money?'

He hauled out his wallet. 'Three hundred and eighty marks.'

'Lend me two hundred and fifty. You'll get it back,' I said.

I matched his bundle with one of my own, and went to give Suzi her fee. She was slicing what looked like a succulent young chicken.

'Are you sure you cannot stay? There's plenty here for *all* of us . . .'

'It looks delicious,' I said, 'but really, no. We must be going.'

'When shall I see you?' she said.

'I've made a note of your number. I'll be giving you a ring.'

'Take care of yourselves.'

'Don't worry, we will.'

'So. *Aufweidersehen.*'

I told Mackenzie to drive us slowly down Cuxhaven Allee, then west along the Reeperbahn. As he drove, I brought him up to date. When I'd finished, he shook his head.

'The cousins are going to be fizzing mad.'

'So what? Let the bastards fizz. It's the sods in our own lot that I'm worried about.'

'Quite. How can they treat us this way?'

'The Section isn't the be-all and end-all. We're an odd-job outfit, Jock.'

'And the Man?'

'Oh, he's pretty autonomous within certain limits, but that's as far as it goes. You might say he's a sort of sub-contractor employed by the powers-that-be to take on the less-delightful assignments. We're not among the élite, we're only the poor bloody infantry.'

'Surely that which we do is worth while?'

'Don't get me wrong. I'm not knocking it, lad, and I'm not trying to talk the job down. But you might as well get wise to the fact that we're not at the top of the tree.'

'But with people like you, and Mr McGowan – '

'He's in a class of his own. Which reminds me: stop at the nearest phone box, and let me have all your loose change.'

Thanks to the marvels of present-day technology, I was able to dial straight through, and he might have been speaking from just across town. He came over loud and clear.

'Charlie?'

'Yes, How's it going?'

'Not too well,' I said. 'Would you believe we've been set up?'

He paused, but not for long.

'Who by?'

'The fat man.'

'D'you know what you're saying?'

'I bloodywell ought to,' I said, 'seeing as I was the one who got caught in the middle!'

'Go on, then, tell me,' he said.

I kept it brief, but with all the essentials, not naming any names and avoiding the use of specifics.

'Suffering Jesus!' he said. 'This sounds like an all-time balls-up!'

'Look – I hope you're not blaming me.'

'No. How do you rate your chances?'

'Of getting him back, you mean? No more than fifty-fifty – but what would I do with him *then*? That's why I'm phoning, for Christ's sake! I'm not going to win this race just to hand the first prize to the fat man!'

'All right, keep your hair on,' he said. 'I'm thinking . . .'

'Well, you'd better think fast. I'm running out of coins.'

'First thing I'll do is talk to the Man – God, but you'd better be sure!'

'Charlie, I'm *sure*.'

'Fair enough, I believe you. Ring me back in an hour.'

I hung up, and scooped what remained of my coins from off the top of the box, and took a good look all around before I got back in the car.

Mackenzie started the engine. 'Where to now?' he said.

'Nowhere. You had your lunch yet?'

'No.'

'Nor have I, so let's get some scoff. We'll try that place over there.'

'It looks expensive . . .'

'Screw the expense. What's it say? *Car park at rear.* Drop me off before you go round, and I'll get some drinks lined up.'

'I'd like – '

'Don't tell me. Martini and soda.'

'Ice and lemon,' he said.

143

Mackenzie slit his fat grilled trout along the dorsal bone, and de-fleshed its flanks with the skill of a surgeon.

'Mmm . . . this is good,' he said.

'At these prices, it had better be good. You got your credit card?'

'Don't tell me yours is at the bottom of the Baltic!'

'No, it's not,' I said, 'but I've had to buy shoes, and I still need a raincoat, and those bastards down in Accounts – '

'Never mind. How's the tournedos?'

'Just what I needed,' I said. 'Look – are you sure you won't have any wine? Claret with trout won't harm . . .'

'It's not that,' he said, 'I just don't, at lunch-time.'

'Keep it up, then,' I said. 'Drink is the root of all evil.'

'I always thought it was money.'

'Yes, but what can the vintners buy – '

' – one half so precious as the goods they sell?'

'Surprised I once read a book?' He coloured, because he *had* looked surprised. 'What about a pudding?' I said.

'Er, have we got time?'

'Why not? An army marches on its stomach.'

'Napoleon,' he said.

'Napoleon, my foot. It was Julius Caesar.'

'Does that mean you've read *two* books?' he said.

I returned his grin. 'You chosen yet?'

'Yes. I'd like some chocolate ice-cream.'

The Scots are voracious eaters of sweet things. I ordered biscuits and cheese, and cut myself a chunk of smoked Austrian. After the coffee came, I looked at my watch. Eight minutes to go.

'Look, I'll leave you to pay the bill. You can pick me up across at the phone box.'

'Roger.'

I asked the waiter for change, and went out and did some more long-distance dialling.

144

'Listen,' said Charlie, 'the Man's upset.'

'Not with me, I hope?'

'No. The fat man's dropped himself right in the khaki. He's getting the hard goodbye.'

'I bleed for him, but where's that leave us?'

'He wants you to follow it through. He's having words in various ears, and he's sending the 125. It'll be at Fulsbüttel airport at five this afternoon, and it's going to stay there as long as it takes.'

'As long as it takes to what?'

'Just listen. When you get our man –'

'*If* we get him, you mean.'

' – ring Sam at the airport hotel, and he'll tell you how to get through the checks.'

'It doesn't look too good, Chas,' I said.

'For Christ's sake get on with it, Farrow!'

'Charlie – *a sailor's farewell!*'

The old part of Blankanese, built on Falkenstein Heights, slopes very steeply down to the river, but the less-ancient top of the town is like any other of the Hamburg suburbs. We found a vacant space, and parked by the S-bahn station and got out and locked up the car. Now, a pale sun shone in a watery sky. The rain clouds had drifted away, and Mackenzie shed his dark blue Burberry.

'Where do we start?' he said.

'We make a bee-line straight for the hill. She'd have run the shortest way. We're looking for a small thatched house with a monkey-puzzle tree.'

Our search dragged on for more than an hour. The whole of Falkenstein Heights is a tortuous warren of pathways and steps which twist and turn down the hill, around and between the picturesque houses. To live there, one had to be fit, and I wondered what the burghers would do should there ever be a fire. Many of the

145

houses were timbered, and most were also thatched, and by the time we found our monkey-puzzle tree my shins were stiff and sore. The square little house with its patch of garden was surrounded by a hedge in which was set a white-painted gate. We walked up the narrow stone path, and I used the brass fox-head knocker to rap on the iron-studded door. The house seemed still and empty, just as I thought it would be. We were shielded from any prying eyes by a tiny windowless porch. I nodded at Mackenzie.

'Do your stuff, Jock,' I said.

He did the old lock in under a minute, then used his credit card to ease back the snib of the ill-fitting Yale. That door was a piece of cake. Inside, there were signs of a hurried departure. All three beds were unmade, and the doors of wardrobes and cupboards hung open. We made a quick search of the place, ending up in the neat tiled kitchen. I looked inside the fridge. It was quite well stocked with a variety of foods, including some fillets of fish and a sizable uncooked chicken. There were eggs, and and two cartons of milk, one of them unopened.

'Look at this lot,' I said.

Mackenzie peered over my shoulder. 'Good Lord, there's enough there to last for days. I wonder why they didn't take it with them, they've taken everything else!'

'Yes. Doesn't that strike you as rather strange?'

'What – the fact that they didn't take the food?'

'No, the fact that they've taken *everything* else, except the furniture.' There wasn't one single personal item any-where in the house. No books, no papers, no clothing at all – not even a pair of old socks.'

'Yet, we know they must have left in a hurry . . .'

'Go on, Sherlock,' I said.

'. . . so there couldn't have been very much to take.'

'What does that suggest?'

'This isn't their home. It's not where they live.'

'I knew you'd get it,' I said. 'Come on, let's go and talk to the next-door neighbour.'

The neighbour turned out to be a widow not quite so young as she looked, but older than she cared to appear. Had Mackenzie not been there, I'm sure she'd have settled for me, and given another time and place, I might have settled for her. Unlike the majority of German matrons, she was really quite petite. There was something she hungered for other than cream cakes. When she saw who had knocked on her door, she smoothed the skirt down over her hips.

'*Guten abend*,' she said.

I fired the opening sally. '*Guten abend, gnädige Frau.* I wonder if you'd mind telling us something about the cottage next door? We are looking for a place to rent, and – '

She stood back. 'Of course, do come in.' She showed us into a pleasant little room, invited us to sit down, and asked if we'd like a cup of coffee. 'I've just made a pot,' she said.

'How very kind.'

'Excuse me, I'll be back in a minute or two.'

The coffee was a Viennese mixture, and very good indeed. She served it to us with tiny sweetmeats made from marzipan, and once we were settled: 'Now,' she went on, 'what can I do for you?'

The loaded question, directed at Mackenzie, made him blush to the roots of his hair. He cleared his throat.

'Well, my friend and I are interested – '

'Yes,' I butted in, 'we called to make inquiries, but there seems to be no one at home.'

She lifted one leg across the other, showing a fair pair of knees. 'The cottage is owned by a man called Ropner, who lives in Düsseldorf. He comes up quite often in the summer, but he lets it the rest of the time. As a matter of fact, it's let at the moment. I've seen some people there.'

'Do you know who they are?'

'I'm afraid I don't. I've seen them once or twice, a man and a woman. They come and go. They might be away on the boat.'

'The boat?'

'Herr Ropner's. It's called the *Hildegarde*. He rents it out with the house.'

'I see. Do you have Herr Ropner's address?'

'No, but I know he uses an agent – Herr Koestler, here in town. His office is in Bundestrasse.'

'Would the office be open today?'

'Oh no, I shouldn't think so.'

'That's a pity,' I said. 'We have to move on to Bremen this evening, and I was hoping to fix things today.'

'When would you wish to have the cottage?'

'We'd like it for the month of May – that is, to move in next weekend.'

She shot a coy glance at Mackenzie. 'Would your friend be staying, too?'

The lad used his loaf. 'Oh, yes,' he said quickly.

'I wonder . . .' the woman said '. . . perhaps you could get in touch with Herr Koestler – at his home, I mean.'

'Do you think he would mind talking business on Sunday?'

'Would you like me to ring him, and ask? We know each other fairly well.'

'How kind,' Mackenzie said. 'If it wouldn't be too much trouble.'

'No trouble at all,' she said. She went to a small antique writing desk tucked in a corner of the room, and we watched her dial a number. 'Herr Koestler? This is Eva Rohde . . . yes, I'm fine, thanks – and you? Good. Herr Koestler, can I ask you, please, about the Ropner house? Some very nice people would like to rent it . . .

yes, they are here with me now . . . yes, I know it's Sunday, but they're going on to Bremen tonight, and they were wondering . . . oh, I see . . . yes, I see. What a pity. Yes, I'll tell them . . . not at all. Sorry to have disturbed you . . . yes, I will. Goodbye.' She hung up the phone and turned to us, her mouth an inverted U. 'Herr Koestler says the present let runs to the end of the month, and then it's booked solid throughout the summer by a regular clientele – people who come here year after year.'

'What a shame,' I said. 'I'd set my heart on a cottage here.'

'Oh, you mustn't give up, you know! Herr Koestler asked me to tell you he has others on his books. Blankanese is full of such properties. If only I had more room, I'd go into the letting business myself. Take paying guests, I mean. Some people here make a fortune!'

'Yes, I'm sure they do.'

'Why don't you go and talk with Herr Koestler? He told me he wouldn't mind, seeing as how you are so pressed for time.'

'Do you have his address?'

'No, but it will be in the phone book – wait, I'll get it for you.'

'Oh, please don't go to any more trouble.'

'No trouble at all,' she said. She thumbed through a telephone directory and copied out Koestler's address, and handed me the slip of paper. Then she told us the best way to go, but urged us, first, to have more coffee.

'I wish we had time,' I said. 'You make excellent coffee, Frau Rohde.'

She simpered. 'Thank you, Herr . . .'

'Stroud,' I said.

'You must both come and see me, when you're fixed up.'

149

'We certainly will,' I said, 'won't we, Herr Stude-meyer?'

'Of course,' Mackenzie said, 'we'd be most honoured, *gnädige Frau.*'

She fluttered her lashes at him. 'One gets so lonely, all on one's own.'

'One must do,' Mackenzie said.

I broke it up. 'Thanks again, Frau Rohde. Now, I'm afraid we must go.'

She stood in the doorway and waved to us as Mac-kenzie closed the gate. Once out of sight, round the corner, I nudged him in the ribs.

'You'd a very narrow escape there, Jock. I thought you were going to be raped.'

'Jealous?'

'Too true I was jealous. Frau Rohde's a bit of all right.'

'A little too long in the tooth for me.'

'Bloody rhubarb,' I said. 'You don't know what you're talking about.'

'Are we going to see Koestler?' he said.

I paused at the foot of a steep flight of steps. 'No, we're not,' I said, 'and I'm not going to scale the Eiger again. You go and get the car, and find your way down to the river. Meet me by the boats.'

'The boats?'

'Yes, there's got to be some sort of moorings down there. You'll find them – go on, on your way.'

The little marina for private craft was tucked in the lee of the pier used by passenger steamers. Now that the weather had cleared, there were quite a few owners messing about. I casually asked around until I found one who knew Ropner's boat.

'The *Hildegarde*? Yes,' he said, 'she's out at the moment.'

'˙ ˙ ˙ *ss!* When did she leave?'

'˙ have been lunch-time,' he said. 'She was here

150

when I went up home to eat, but when I came back, she was gone. Are you thinking of hiring her, then?'

'Well, I might be,' I said. 'Depends on what kind of shape she's in.'

'Oh, she's a nice boat,' he said. 'Cabin cruiser, Sea Ranger type.'

'How big is she?' I said.

'Four metres. Petrol engine, so a little bit hungry on juice, but nice and steady. You want her for fishing?'

'That's the general idea. Thanks for the information.'

'Not at all, you're welcome,' he said.

I left him rubbing down his coach-roof, and looked around for the car. It was some time before I spotted it.

'Where've you been, Jock?' I said.

'It's a long way round.'

'Well, never mind. Things are looking up.'

'Did you find the boat?'

'No, I didn't, she's missing from her berth. Listen, let's get out of here.'

'Where to?'

'Back to the top of the town. We've one more call to make, and and then I'll get on to Harvester. I want that shipping list.'

We had to go all the way around the Heights to get back up to the station. The space we had occupied previously was still vacant, and Mackenzie backed us in. I did not relish more footwork, but we took to the streets again.

'What are we looking for this time?'

'A laundry. Nearest one to the house.'

We found it fairly easily. It had a typical jaw-breaking name – *Der Blitzreinigungsanstalten*, dry-cleaners and laundry combined. Not unnaturally, the place was closed. I fixed its location firmly in my mind, and we plodded back to the car.

'Are you sure you don't want us to call on Koestler – to find out who rented the house?'

'They'd do it through a cut-out, and they'd use a phoney name.'

'Wouldn't the agent want references?'

'Not if they paid in advance.'

'They'd probably use a phoney name at the laundry.'

'Yes,' I said, 'I know, but it's worth a try. We'll check tomorrow. Let's get back to the car.'

Before we left Blankanese, I telephoned Harvester.

'Farrow?' he said. 'Where the hell have you been?'

'Chasing wild geese,' I said. 'You got that shipping list for us?'

'Yes, I have,' he said.

'I also want some money. I need a thousand marks.'

'Good God, man! Don't you realize it's Sunday?'

'If you tell me that one more time, I'll lose my cool. I mean it.'

'How soon do you want it, then?'

'Half an hour from now.'

'It'll take a good hour. I'll be at the office.'

'No, make it the Schloss Hotel. Ask for Stroud, room 337.'

He sighed. 'Oh, very well.'

We were back at the Schloss inside the half-hour, and went straight up to my room. I rearranged the pillows, and sat on the bed. Mackenzie took the armchair.

'Does Mr Harvester know that we know?'

'Not officially,' I said. 'But he's nobody's fool, so he'll know we suspect. He'll be wary from now on.'

'It puts us in an awkward position.'

'Does it hell as like. He's the one in the awkward position. We can feed him a load of old cods, and he's
tion but to lap it all up, just in case it might be

152

'Are you going to tell him we've got the girl?'

'Not bloody likely!' I said. 'Let him find out from the cousins. They'll be screaming blue murder by now.'

'The Man might be forced to co-operate with them.'

'I hardly think so,' I said. 'Now that he knows they made fools of us all, the old sod will dig in his heels and tell CIS to get knotted.'

'But won't he be forced, in the end?'

'No doubt, but he'll see that we're given a chance to complete our assignment *first* – hang on, now, I want to study form.'

'The MOSSAD people?'

'Yes.'

There were only two females on the list, and both were much too young to be the woman described by the girl. The man could have been any one of several. I put the list away.

'I've been thinking,' said Mackenzie.

'What about?' I said.

'They might have moved Jagersberg out by car.'

'I very much doubt that,' I said. 'By now, the cousins will have piled on the pressure. The entire *Staatspolizei*, plus their mates in the BND, will be buzzing around like blue-arsed flies. There won't be an airport, a road, or a dock – '

'Including Hamburg,' he said.

'Especially including Hamburg.'

'And especially Israeli ships. So how the blazes – '

'Listen . . .' I said. I told him how I thought they would try it.

'Ah, I see,' he said. 'So it's all going to hinge on the shipping movements.'

'Not all of it,' I said. 'We can't afford to sit on arses and gamble on that alone. MOSSAD will about Fischer by now, and they know that the h blown, so we can't be certain what they might need to pursue every lead, and hope we come up with the right one.'

Just then, the telephone rang. I reached across and grabbed the receiver.

'All right, send him up.'

'Harvester?'

'You've got it. Just stay right where you are, and make like the three wise monkeys.'

'I'll go get a chair from my room.'

Percy arrived as Mackenzie came back, lugging an extra chair. Once the door had closed behind him, Harvester wasted no time.

'Now look here, Farrow, what's going on?'

'Sit down, Percy,' I said. 'Did you bring the list, and the money?'

'Of course I did!' he said. He hauled out a long brown envelope and tossed it on to the bed. 'You'll have to sign for the cash, you know.'

'Naturally,' I said, 'I wouldn't want you to be stuck for it, mate.'

'What's happening?' he asked again.

'Happening?' I said. 'Why, nothing.'

'Don't give me that,' he said. 'There's talk of shooting having gone on.'

'Shooting? What shooting?' I said. I could feel the heavy VP-70 digging into my side.

'You know the rule about carrying weapons – '

'on a minute!' I said. 'Who says we're carrying

nobody,' he said. 'But shots were fired

said. 'But you already knew

have it. Get it, Mackenzie,' I

154

When Mackenzie had left the room, Harvester rounded on me. 'Just what the hell are you playing at, Farrow?'

'Now look here, Percy,' I said, 'stop talking in bloody riddles.'

'You know damn well what I mean. The cousins have filed a strong complaint. They say that you and Mackenzie beat up one of their men.'

'Me and Mackenzie? You've got to be kidding!'

'The descriptions fit,' he said, 'and so does the car registration number.'

'They're putting you on, Perce,' I said. 'You know what devious bastards they are.'

'Come off it, Farrow,' he said. 'Why should they invent such a story? What would be the point?'

'Christ knows. Anyway, thanks for the money.'

'Where have you been all day?'

'I wouldn't want to bore you with it.'

'I wouldn't *be* bored,' he said.

'No, but I would. To tell the truth, it was all just a waste of time.'

'I see,' he said stiffly. 'You're not going to tell me.'

'I knew you'd catch on,' I said.

'I could have you pulled out of Hamburg tonight!'

'Tell you what, Percy,' I said, 'do me a favour. Do it. I'll be very damned glad to get home.'

He struggled to heave himself out of the chair. 'Don't leap away,' I said. 'Mackenzie will be back in a minute.'

'You think you're smart, Farrow,' he said, 'but let me tell you something. *I* was with the Section before you – '

'Oh, stuff it!' I said. 'I don't give a toss about that sort of crud.'

He lumbered, red-faced, to the door. Just as Mackenzie came back with the rifle. He snatched at the leather case, and stormed away down the corridor w

'Oh dear,' Mackenzie said, 'I'd say at a guess annoyed our large friend.'

'Bollocks to him,' I said, 'he's the least of our worries now. Come in, and shut the door, and we'll run a check on the shipping forecast.'

'Before we do that,' he said, 'there's something I'd better tell you.'

'Well, go on, then,' I said.

'When I went to the car to get the Husqvarna, some chap was just walking away.'

'What – away from the car?'

'That's right.'

'Did he see you?'

'Not at first,' he said. 'You remember we parked at the end of the garage furthest away from the lift? Well, I don't think he heard the doors slide open. There were plenty of cars in between – '

'You're sure he was moving away from *our* car?'

'Pretty sure,' he said. 'If it wasn't ours, it was the next one.'

'Do you think he was trying to break in?'

'I really don't know, I just saw him move off.'

'What happened when *he* saw *you*?'

'He just kept on walking up the ramp, heading for the street. I went up to a different car, and pretended to check the boot.'

'Well, I'll tell you something,' I said, 'we're going to check more than the boot before we start up that Ford

wouldn't – '

dywell would, you know. That shower lock. Anyway, forget it for now. Let's

one. Only five ships in all.
day with a cargo of citrus
uple of days to discharge. Of
ie *Jepthah*, was due to run for
of timber for Haifa. There is

156

very little trade between West Germany and Israel, and each of the other three ships was sailing out under ballast to take on cargoes elsewhere. One of them to London, and two to Rotterdam. The *Jepthah* was due to leave harbour on Monday, at four in the afternoon.

'. . . so it rather looks like the *Jepthah*, Mackenzie.'

'The cousins will figure that, too, and MOSSAD will figure they've figured it.'

'Indubitably,' I said. Not a bad word for a rainy Sunday. 'But we, my young friend,' I went on, 'are one step ahead of the buggers, aren't we?'

'Are we? I hope so,' he said.

'You just trust your uncle Marcus. Now then, what's the hour?'

'Er . . . ten to seven.'

'I thought it must be. It's noggins time,' I said. 'Followed by a spot of sustenance – what?'

'I'll just freshen up, then,' he said.

'Do that. I'll meet you down in the bar.'

'I won't be long,' he said.

'Aren't you forgetting something?'

'Oh, yes, the chair,' he said.

'Ever do a car-check before, Mackenzie?'

'Yes, up in Sutherland,' he said.

'Right then, sunshine, give me the keys, and you take a look underneath.'

I checked all the doors, then released the bonnet and did the bonnet lid. There was nothing wired up to the starter, and nothing else I could see. But when I felt under the front off-side wheel arch my fingers encountered a knob which had nothing to do with th bodywork. One hard push, and the knob fell away, an straightened up with the thing in my hand. Macke got up off the floor, and took off his raincoat and br at the dirt.

'Nothing. She's clean,' he said.

'She is *now*.' I showed him the neat little bleeper.

'Where did you find that?' he said.

'Clamped by its magnet, under the wheel arch.'

'I was right after all, then,' he said. 'Lucky you sent me to get the Husqvarna.'

'Isn't it, though?' I said. I crouched by the wheel, and replanted the bug. Mackenzie frowned at me.

'What's the idea of putting it back?'

'We're going to box clever,' I said, 'let them think we don't know it's there.'

'But they'll tail us wherever we go!'

'Only so long as we want them to. They'll know about Wintzer, of course, because Harvester will have told them, but I don't want them knowing that we know that they know. Got it?'

'I think so,' he said, 'but why are we bothering with Wintzer at all?'

'Christ, I've just told you,' I said. 'We're feeding the sods a big fat red herring.'

'Ah,' he said, 'I see.'

'Right, you get into the back of the car and sit on the floor, out of sight. We don't know how many men Toomey's got, but if he thinks you're elsewhere, he'll have to spread them thin on the ground.'

'Divide and conquer?'

'~ect.'

'~esar?'

'~n,' he said.

'~ day, is equally impressive by
~ceful spires are bathed in
~tic pile of the *Rathaus* is
~ almost-ethereal soft green
~rough the town I kept an eye
conscious all the time of the

little transmitter beaming out its message. There were always cars behind, but I couldn't pick out any particular one which might be following me. With the bug, they wouldn't need to stay close. I tracked the big clear signs until I was on the Federal Highway number 433, and stopped when I got to Langenhorn in order to ask the way.

There, I found Wintzer's house easily. It lay back off a long straight road which seemed to run through a forest of pines, but every forty or fifty metres a track ran off through the trees, each one marked by a numbered signpost. Wintzer's was 142. The footpaths on either side of the road were more than eight feet wide, and the Germans habitually park on their footpaths. I rolled on past Wintzer's drive, then bumped the Ford up over the kerb and switched off all the lights. There weren't any street-lamps, and I couldn't see a thing. As I waited for my eyes to adjust:

'All right, Mackenzie,' I said, 'out you get, and lose yourself.'

'What do you want me to do?'

'Just keep your beady eyes open, boy.'

I heard the snap of the latch, then the click of the door as he closed it behind him. I lingered a minute or so, then quit the car and locked up all round. The edge of the hard sandy footpath was marked by a four-foot fence of plastic-covered heavy wire netting. I felt my way along it until I came to the signpost, then turned into Wintzer's drive, stepping cautiously in the darkness. I must have walked fifty yards before I discerned the light from his porch lamp filtering through the trees, light which grew progressively stronger as I rounded a sweeping cur. The house itself, which was big and square, had a hung mansard roof broken by large dormer win four on either side. The main door, reached b stone steps, fronted a long patio on which sto urns filled with wallflowers. Their heavy scent drenched the air, reminding me of my flower troughs at home. My long double ring at the bell was answered by a uniformed maid. She looked me up and down.

'*Bitte, mein Herr?*'

'Is Herr Wintzer at home?'

'I will see. Who is calling?' she said.

'Oh, he doesn't know me, my name is Stroud,' I said. 'I'm here on holiday.'

'Please wait.'

She did not ask me in, and I stood there cooling my heels on the porch while three or four minutes dragged by. Then the door swung open again.

'*Ja – was ist?*' he said.

He was one of your forthright, no-nonsense people who start as they mean to go on. I topped him by several inches, but he looked a deal heavier than me, and not very much of it muscle. Hardly a yachting type. He probably had minions to crew for him, and saw about as much of the sea as could gently be scanned from the estuary. He was sporting a quilted smoking jacket, silk muffler at his throat. His plump cheeks were marbled by broken veins. He had rather protuberant eyes, and short straight hair the colour of porridge.

'Herr Wintzer?'

'...s, yes,' he said. 'Please be brief, I am busy.'

' not ask me in. I could feel warm air from the

ˋout my car – that is, the car I hired

ˇhat the hell are you raving

ₙe car was parked up in ɔmenade. When I went to ᴠas staved in.'

160

'For God's sake, man, explain yourself! What has this got to do with me?'

'I was told that the damage had been done by some people seen to be leaving your boat – you do own the *Übermensche*, don't you?'

'Yes, I do,' he said, 'but damage your car? What absolute rubbish! None of us left the boat until after ten o'clock this morning! Look here – is this some kind of joke?'

'Joke?' I said.

'Yes, stupid joke! I've a good mind to call the police!'

'I am only trying, Herr Wintzer – '

'Listen to me,' he said. He indexed-fingered me hard in the breast bone, 'I have influence in Hamburg, you hear? If I'm bothered by any more of you people, I'll . . . well, you just wait and see!'

With that, he slammed the door in my face, and I heard a bolt rattle home. I wondered what sort of trumped-up yarn the cousins had spun to him. Probably no less unlikely than my own. I turned away from the place and went down the steps and set off up the drive. It was cold. I was missing my coat. I rounded the bend into deeper darkness. A car's headlights flashed by on the road, affording me a glimpse of the gap in the trees which flanked the drive. I was afforded no glimpse of the pair who attacked me until it was much too late.

The sad fact is, I am slowing down. I heard the fast scrabble of feet, and tried to turn, but I couldn't be sure from which direction they came. I took a hard jolt to the side of my neck, another one under the heart, and then I went down and the boot came in.

'That's enough,' somebody said, and the somebody who said it hunkered down by my side and dragged the pistol out of my waistband. 'Get up, you Limey turd.' I lay there with my face in the gravel, trying to get back my breath. 'You heard me, Farrow – up on your feet!'

'Farrow, is it?' I said. 'You're supposed to think my name's Nelson, same as it was in Spain.'

'Ah, you remember me, do you?'

'Who could forget you,' I said.

'Let me get him up for you, Francis. I owe this shit-heel a few.'

Now I knew who the other one was. I pushed myself up on my knees, then into a crouch, with my feet set firm.

'Don't try it,' Toomey said, 'or we'll *really* give you the business.'

They were looking for an excuse, and two professionals up against one will beat him any day. Especially when the two are young, and the one is past his prime and feeling knackered into the bargain. So I came up nice and slow, and Toomey rammed the pistol muzzle into one of my vertebrae.

'Head for the road – and don't make me waste you.'

'Give over, you pillock,' I said, 'you've been watching too much television.'

'A smart-ass,' the other one said. 'Let me lean on him, Francis.'

'Later, Bob,' Toomey said. 'Wait till we get him some-where more private.'

'Your place, or mine?' I said.

'I told you to move it, Farrow!'

'Temper, temper!' I said. 'You're setting junior a bad example.'

They herded me up to their car, which had been backed into the top of the driveway, hard up alongside the trees. The young one opened both offside doors, and slid in under the wheel, and quickly wound his window down. Toomey pushed me into the back and pressed in beside me, holding the pistol rammed against my side.

Where the hell was Mackenzie.

'Let's go, Bob,' Toomey said.

162

Our driver flipped on his sidelights, and reached for the ignition key.

'*Touch that starter, I'll blow your head off!*'

The fist which thrust over the sill was wrapped around a Smith & Wesson. Toomey's protégé froze, with his hand on the key and his head on one side as the foresight ground in his ear. Mackenzie was crouched below the level of the sill of the driver's door, so that only his forearm was visible. The Sutherland training, no doubt. Endless seconds of loaded silence. Finally, Toomey said:

'It's a stand-off.'

'Stand-off, my arse!' I said. 'My partner shoots Robert, and then he shoots Francis.'

'By which time, Francis shoots you. So call him off!'

'He'd take no notice,' I said. 'He's headstrong. It's his one big failing – isn't it, you wilful young sod?'

Mackenzie must have eased down on the handle. Suddenly, he flung back the door and grabbed at the driver and caught him good and dragged him down out of the car.

'For Christ's sake, Francis – cool it!'

It came as a strangled yell. Then we heard Mackenzie call out.

'You in the car!' he said. 'Give up the gun, or this one gets it!'

'Face up to it, Toomey,' I said. 'They won't even give you a decent funeral.'

'You bloody bastard!' he said.

'Come, now,' I said, 'don't be bitter.'

'There'll be another day!'

It was then that I knew we had him. I groped around at my side, and he let me take back the VP-70.

'Thank you, Francis,' I said. 'We didn't really want any shooting, did we? Isn't it better this way?'

'I'll get you yet, you no-account asshole!'

'Who knows what the future might bring?' I made him

163

raise his left arm a little, and emptied his shoulder rig. 'Now . . . out you get . . . that's it, nice and easy – how's yours, Mackenzie?' I said.

'He's lying here so peaceful, he could be asleep.'

'Probably just napping,' I said. 'Any more playthings about his person?'

'I've taken it from him,' he said. 'Incidentally, I let all their tyres down.'

'Hear that, Toomey?' I said. 'I told you he was a rascal.'

'Laugh while you can,' Toomey said.

'If there's one thing I hate, it's rancour. Come on, Mackenzie,' I said, 'it's way past your bedtime. Say good night.'

'Good night, chaps,' Mackenzie said.

As we backed off I called out to Toomey. 'Just to show there's no ill-feeling, we'll leave your guns by the gate. Look for them under the signpost.'

He did not deign to reply. Back at the car, I removed the bug and hurled it into the trees.

'Shall I drive?' asked Mackenzie.

'Why not?' I gave him the keys.

'Back to the Schloss?'

'Yes, to pick up our gear. I think we'd better move on. And get your foot down, I don't want to linger.'

As Mackenzie climbed up through the gears, 'Where are we moving on *to*?' he said.

'An empty house I know.'

'Not the one in Blankanese!'

'How did you guess, lad?' I said.

Monday

'I don't think I've ever eaten fish for breakfast.

'Come off it, you must have had kippers.'

'No, honestly. Never,' he said.

'You haven't lived. Now, don't just stand there, get the kettle on. Then you can set the table.'

'Where's the silverware?'

'What are you on about – *silverware*? Put out some knives and forks, they're in that drawer beside the sink . . . oh, Jesus, there isn't any bread!'

'Here's a packet of those Jewish biscuit things.'

'Bring 'em out, they'll do. Hurry up with the tea, this is almost ready.'

'What about cornflakes?' he said.

'Never mind cornflakes, do some plates. Heat them under the grill.'

'Which is the grill?'

'Christ Almighty! Where have you been all your life? On second thoughts, don't answer that.'

'It smells very good,' he said.

'Jock,' I said, 'you're a source of delight. Hand me that lemon, please. Pity we don't have any white grapes.'

'What – for sole bonne femme?'

'Well, plaice bonne femme would be more like it.'

'Gosh, it does smell good,' he said.

'You said that before. Now, sit yourself down – no, get the butter out first. It's in the fridge. That's the fridge, over there.'

'You're putting me on,' he said.

'Never! Here, get stuck into that lot.'

'This is really delicious,' he said.

'Of course it's delicious. I'm not just a pretty face.'

As we ate, I told Mackenzie what I was planning to do.

'Do you think we'll be able to pull it off?'

'We can give it a bloody good try.'

'Where are we going to get the boat?'

'Hire it, if we can. If not, we shall just have to nick one.'

'The owner might sound the alarm, and it's seventy miles to the mouth of the Elbe. They'd spot us long before – '

'That's only if we're forced to nick one – *and* if we nicked it from here.'

'Where else could we find one?'

'Cuxhaven, lad. You ought to have realized that.'

'So you think they'll transfer Jagersberg when the *Jepthah* is well out at sea?'

'Assuming they do intend to put him aboard the *Jepthah*, yes. They certainly won't try it in the docks, and I don't think they'll try it in the river. They'll wait until the *Jepthah*'s a good twelve miles off shore.'

'We're taking a hell of a gamble. What if we're wrong?' he said.

'If we're wrong, we've had it. We'll just head for home.'

'With my first real job a failure.'

'Rubbish. Anyway, it's not *your* job, and I just couldn't care less.'

'I think you could.'

'Oh, do you.'

'Yes.'

'Well, start the washing up. I want to make a couple of phone calls.'

I telephoned Suzi first, and asked her how the girl was faring.

'Oh, she's much better,' she said. 'We're just about to have breakfast.'

'Splendid. Look,' I said, 'I'd better have a word with her.'

'Just a moment, I'll put her on.'

'Ilse?'

'Yes.'

'How are you feeling?'

'I'm all right, now,' she said. 'Have you any news of my – '

'Careful! Don't talk, just listen,' I said. 'If all goes well, we'll be picking you up some time late tonight.'

'What about my . . .'

'Yes, I hope he'll be with us. You're not to worry, you hear? Stay indoors, and keep out of sight. Suzi will look after you, and if there's anything you want, just ask her for it. Yes, I will . . . see you later . . . goodbye.'

The hotel people had to fetch Harvey out of the dining room.

'Sam?'

'Hey, Marcus! Where are you, old buddy?'

'That doesn't matter,' I said. 'What's the form for this exit?'

'Easy as pee-ing,' he said. 'You let me have half an hour's notice, then come in at gate number eight – that's a freight gate at the south-west corner, near the big Al Italia sign.'

'You're sure there will be no hold-up?'

'Quite sure. The Man's had a word. Seems that somebody owes him a favour. What time do you think you'll arrive?'

'I don't know, it could be the early hours. You'll just have to stand by,' I said.

'No problem. See you when you get here.'

We left the house more or less as we'd found it, and were up at the Blankanese laundry soon after it opened, at nine. The manageress was helpful. I spun her a fancy yarn about a mix-up of identical luggage.

'. . . nothing of any great value, just clothes, you understand.'

'Forgive me, *mein Herr*, but I do not – '

'I'm coming to that,' I said. 'I realized when we were off the train that I had the wrong suitcase, you see, and ran after the lady who had taken mine by mistake. I saw her getting into a taxi – this was yesterday – but was just too late to catch her. However, I spoke to the porter who had helped her with her things, and he told me he'd heard her tell the driver to take her to Blankanese. Well, I opened her suitcase to see whether I could find any address or identification. I couldn't, but several items of clothing bore the same laundry mark, and I thought I might perhaps trace her that way.'

'Ah, I see,' she said. 'Well, if we can help you . . .'

'Here's the number,' I said. 'I wrote it down on a piece of paper.'

She looked at the number I'd written down, and started to shake her head. 'No, that is not from Blankanese – '

'Isn't it? Damn!' I said.

' – no, it's from one of our other branches. Ours is a big firm, you see. We have depots all over the Hamburg area.' Her pink-painted fingernail moved along the letters and numerals. 'This, BM, is for *Blitzreinigungsanstalten* and this, 792, is the customer's own number. The final two letters denote the branch.'

'Why, that's terrific!' I said. 'Can you tell me which branch SU stands for?'

'No, but if you'd care to wait a few minutes, I will telephone head office. All the records are there.'

'Fräulein, how very kind,' I said.

'Excuse me, I won't be long.' She went off into the nether regions, leaving an assistant in charge, and seemed to be gone for quite some time. When at last she came back to the counter, she was beaming all over her face. 'Got it! The lady you are looking for is Frau or Fräulein Parbs, and the SU stands for Schulau. I asked for the address. It's Bismarckstrasse, thirty.'

'Marvellous!' I said. 'Fräulein, how can I thank you?'

'Please, it was nothing,' she said. 'I'm only too glad we were able to help you.'

Just how much she helped us, that girl will never know. After leaving the laundry, we sought out a decent men's outfitters and I bought myself a coat. A dark blue English Burberry.

'Very smart,' Mackenzie said.

'Don't let old Witherspoon hear you say that or he'll veto the bloody expense. He's going to query it, anyway.'

'But surely, even Accounts – '

'You don't know the bastards like I do, Jock. Anyway, never mind. Let's get down to Schulau.'

'Are the Parbs on Harvester's list?'

'No, but they wouldn't be, would they? They'd use sleepers for a job like this, and thank God for that. The cousins won't know them.'

'So it looks like we're home and dry.'

'I wouldn't be too sure, but it's certainly hopeful. Here, you drive,' I said.

Schulau is a pleasant spot on the northern bank of the Elbe, one of several upper-class suburbs which fringe the riverside. It rather reminded me of Marlowe. Same sort of properties there, many with land running down to the water. The river is wider, of course, and carries a lot of shipping. We parked near the centre of town, and walked past the house in Bismarckstrasse. It was a residential backwater of good detached post-war houses interspersed with small blocks of flats, each on its own little section of land. There was a newish Opel Kadet in the driveway. We strolled by on the opposite side, taking care not to show any undue interest. The house was too far away from the river to have its own landing stage, so we went on to comb the moorings in search of the *Hildegarde*. We found her almost too easily.

'What now?' Mackenzie said.

I nodded towards a handy bar on the other side of the road. 'I think we've earned ourselves a drink.'

'It's only eleven o'clock.'

'I don't give a monkey's what time it is. You please yourself,' I said.

The barman said he had no Glenmorangie, so I settled for a beer. Mackenzie ordered coffee. We sat at a table beside a window through which we could just see the boat. There seemed to be no sign of life on board. I packed and lit a pipe, and drank two more beers. Mackenzie sipped coffee. The bar began to fill up, and at half past twelve I made a decision.

'Listen, Mackenzie,' I said, 'I'm going to take a look at her.'

'Is that wise?' he said. 'Suppose they come whilst you're still on board?'

'Just too bad,' I said.

'I thought we were going to hire a boat?'

'We don't need one now, do we?' I said. 'If they're planning to use the *Hildegarde* –'

'Suppose they aren't?' he said.

'Why else would they berth her in Schulau?'

'Perhaps they brought Jagersberg down in her.'

'Hardly, Mackenzie. No, having regard to the fact that he's ill, they'd have brought him down by car.'

'Do you really think they've got him in that house?'

'I'm betting on it,' I said. 'Otherwise, it's a North Sea job, and *that*, I can do without.'

'If he *is* in the house, why don't we go get him?'

'What, in broad daylight?' I said, 'with the neighbours peeking through their curtains? No, we'll wait until dark.'

'How do you reckon the timing, then?'

'Well, the *Jepthah* is due to leave harbour at four o'clock, and she won't do more than ten knots in the river – twelve at very most – so it's going to be around midnight before she hits the open sea.'

'What's about the speed of the *Hildegarde*?'

'Oh, she'll do twenty,' I said, 'so I figure they'll leave around half past seven, possibly eight o'clock. They won't want to hang about in the river.'

'I still think –'

'Well, don't,' I said. 'We're going to do it nice and quiet.'

'Shouldn't we be watching the house?'

'We can't, without running the risk of being spotted. We haven't got the gear. There's just no way we can mount a stake-out.'

'It's terribly risky,' he said.

'So is crossing the road, lad. But there's only two of us here, and we can't be in both places at once – not to do any good. Once we split up, we can't communicate quickly.'

'Yes, I see what you mean. So we put all our eggs in the *Hildegarde* basket?'

'You've finally grasped it,' I said.

I was sure that, under the circumstances, it was the best thing for us to do. It left us with two fall-back positions. If Jagersberg's abductors had not brought him to the boat by eight o'clock, I meant to do the house on Bismarckstrasse. Should there be no one at home, it would mean a drive down to Cuxhaven, the getting of a boat, then playing cat and mouse with the *Jepthah*. I hoped it would not come to that.

The bar was pervaded by food smells now, as people came in to eat lunch. It was also pervaded by noise. A portly burgher who should have known better was trying to beat the one-armed bandit with the single-minded determination of a Las Vegas matron. The infernal machine was crashing and thudding not four feet away from my ear, and the stacatto clatter as it spewed out coins was getting on my nerves. Precisely the sort of racket I hate. I supped off the last of my beer, and prepared to get the hell out of the place. I was buttoning up my nice new raincoat, when:

'*Look, sir!*' Mackenzie said.

That which he urged me to look at was the metallic-bronze Opel Kadet we had seen in the driveway on Bismarckstrasse. It tooled past the front of the bar, and slowed to turn right on to the strip of hard-standing in front of the moorings. We watched it brake to a halt beside a boat-trailer parked by the little slipway, close to the *Hildegarde*. The man who got out of the car was wearing a waterproof parka, and ankle-length rubber boots. He was fairly tall, about five foot ten, dark, and medium build. He opened the Opel's boot, gathered up a bundle of folded blankets, and carried them on to the boat. He dumped the blankets on top of the coach-roof while he unlocked the cabin hatch, then pulled them down and took them inside. I nudged Mackenzie's arm.

'Get me another beer, Jock.'

The man – I assumed it was Parbs – was in the boat no more than a minute before climbing back up to the car. He hauled out four five-gallon jerry cans, obviously full, and stowed them in the well of the boat. This done, he ducked back into the cabin, and was out of sight for some time. All of twenty minutes. When he came out again, we saw him close and lock the hatch. Then he returned to the car, and drove away without looking back.

'Confirmation, Jock,' I said. 'He's taken on extra fuel.'

'Looks rather like it,' he said. 'Do you still intend to go on board?'

172

'No need to, now,' I said. 'He might as well have given it to us in writing.'

'Yes, I must agree.'

'Very good of you. Fancy a morsel of lunch?'

'There's a restaurant just down the road.'

'You're getting good at restaurants.'

'Yes, I'm learning fast,' he said. 'What do we do when we've eaten?'

'We watch, and wait,' I said.

I spent most of the afternoon catching up on my sleep, slumped in the back of the car. When Mackenzie woke me at seven o'clock the windows were all steamed up, and the lights outside seemed diffused and opaque. I got out of the car to stretch my cramped limbs. The chill night air hit me hard, and prompted a sudden sharp call of nature. I walked away from the street lights, towards the water's edge and down the concrete ramp of the slipway. As I stood there decently hidden in darkness enjoying blessed relief, a merchantman steamed slowly downstream with her bridge and foc's'le and after-deck picked out in pools of light. I zipped up, shuddering, and buttoned my coat and hurried back to the warmth of the car.

'I think we'd better move this thing, Jock.'

'Yes, I was going to suggest that,' he said. 'We're a little bit conspicuous, now that the other cars have all gone.'

'Right, park over there, in front of the boozer. Make sure you can still see the boat.' As he started the motor and pulled away I hauled out the Heckler & Koch, and checked the action yet again. 'Better check yours, too,' I said.

'Do you think there might be shooting?'

'I don't know, do I?' I said. He backed the car

between two others, and switched the engine off. 'How are we doing for petrol?'

'All right. I topped up yesterday.'

'Good. Now, you know the best way out to the airport?'

'Yes, straight back towards town, then cut up north on the inner ring road.'

'How long will it take us?' I said.

'Oh, forty-five minutes – an hour at most.'

'We've got to stop on the way, and ring Sam Harvey. He needs a half hour's notice.'

'Roger, got it,' he said. 'What's the drill for taking Jagersberg?'

'I'm going on board the boat. When you see them come, get over there fast. I might need some back-up,' I said. 'No shooting unless you absolutely have to.'

'What if they don't show?' he said.

'If they're not here by eight, we'll do the house.'

'Why not do it now?'

'Because I say so. Any questions?'

'No, I don't think so,' he said.

'Okay, then. Keep your eyes peeled.'

As I stepped out of the car again I was tempted to succumb to the beckoning lights of the little bar. A large Scotch would have gone down well. I looked at my watch. There just wasn't time. I nipped across the road and walked beside the row of chain-linked bollards fronting the moorings parking space. It was cold. I could hear the water sucking and lapping around the piles of the landing stage, and the dark row of boats tugged fretfully against their tethering warps. There was a thin layer of mist on the river, and the distant lights on the opposite shore had a curious mirage-like quality. Cars passed along the road, but I was the only pedestrian.

I climbed across the *Hildegarde*'s transom, cautiously feeling my way, and barked my shin on a jerry can. I stooped to feel its weight. It was full, all right, and so were the others. I groped around in the dark, and when I flicked my lighter I saw with some relief that the lock on the hatch was an ordinary Yale-type. So, out with the credit card. I thought at first that I wasn't going to do it. The brass tongue refused to budge, and the plastic sheet buckled under my fingers. I turned the card around and eased it in sideways and pushed with both hands. The snib began then to slide, and I tugged at the hatch and one side swung open. I stumbled down into the cabin and closed the hatch at my back, and paused for some seconds just breathing in darkness before flicking my lighter again.

The cabin layout was typical. Wide seats port and starboard doubled up as bunks. Between them, a bolted-down drop-leaf table. The bunk on the starboard side had been made up with blankets and pillows. The side-screen curtains were drawn. I edged crabwise past the table to get at the narrow door set into the for'ard bulkhead. It was just as I had supposed. The bow-section harboured three compartments. The one on the starboard side housed a midget-sized shower, a wash-hand basin, and a thigh-cramping stainless-steel loo. The sliding door on the port side revealed storage space for clothes, and the V-shaped locker up in the bows held a motley assortment of gear.

I squatted on the deck with my back to the locker, and settled down to wait, holding the pistol between my bent knees. The air in that cramped dark space soon became tainted and stifling. I peered at the face of my watch. The luminous dial glowed faintly green. Twenty-five minutes to eight. After what seemed like half an hour I checked again. It was nearly a quarter-to. I began to be plagued by doubt. At five-to, the doubt intensified. The old wound in my thigh was giving me several kinds of hell. I pulled myself up on my feet, my stiffened joints cracking like pistol shots, to grope for the knob of the door and the top of my skull hit the deck-head.

As I stooped there cursing in the darkness I heard a muffled thud, and the boat pitched very definitely as somebody stepped on board. Mackenzie? No, there were voices. They must have opened the hatch. Stumbling, scuffling noises then, and the boat rolled violently as though a couple of drunks were staggering around in the cabin. I heard a man say something in a language I couldn't understand, and assumed that it must be Hebrew. A woman answered him, then somebody groaned and said, in German:

'Where are you taking me?'

'Just be still,' the woman soothed.

'Let's *all* be still!' I said.

I made quite sure as I opened the door that the first thing they saw was the gun. The duffel-coated woman was bending over the bunk, tucking blankets round Jagersberg. The man was down aft, at the hatch, about to duck out on to the well-deck. They stared at me, faces slack with amazement. I had seen the man once before, when he came to the boat that afternoon. The woman had high cheekbones, and straight dark hair just turning grey.

'You must be the Parbses,' I said.

'What –'

'Come on, you know perfectly well – *Mackenzie*?'

'Right here,' he said. His shape bulked large in the open hatch. He flashed me a white-toothed grin, then stuck the muzzle of the Smith & Wesson into Parbs's left ear and nudged him down, back into the cabin.

'Isn't this cosy?' I said. 'What are we going to do with 'em, Jock?'

'Up to you, sir,' he said.

176

We were speaking in German. 'Well, Parbs?'

'*Scheiss!* Who are you?' he said.

'I don't think that really matters, does it?'

'Listen – we'll do a deal . . .'

'No deals. Jock, frisk the bugger.' Parbs was not carrying a gun. 'All right,' I said, 'now the woman. You, Parbs, stay where you are.'

Mackenzie searched the woman for weapons. 'No, she's clean,' he said.

'Did you feel in her knickers pocket?'

'Pardon?'

'Never mind,' I said, 'just don't take your eyes off her.'

Jagersberg must have been drugged. He lay on his back staring up at the deck-head, a thousand miles away. They probably had him on opiates.

'Wait – let us talk,' Parbs said.

'Shut up!' I squeezed past the table, and menaced him with the gun. 'Start the engine, and get us cast off.'

'Cast off?' Mackenzie said.

'I told you to watch the woman. Go on, Parbs, you heard me!' I said.

The first time Parbs hit the starter the engine spluttered and died, but it picked up at the second attempt and swelled to a throaty roar. I held the pistol on him as he jumped up to let go the warps, then beckoned him back down into the boat.

'Now take her out,' I said.

'In which direction?'

'Just out,' I told him, 'head her into mid-stream, and I'll tell you when to turn down-river.'

He took the small wheel and let in the clutch and we slid past the boat alongside with a groaning and rubbing of fenders. I sat on the seat in the stern, and watched him in the light from the open hatch. As we pulled away from the wharf, he turned his head and said:

177

'Listen – '

'I don't want to listen,' I said. 'And open that throttle, we haven't got all night.'

'Are you going to kill us?' he said.

'Not unless you're naughty.'

'What will you do with us, then?'

'You'll see. Just keep your eyes on the river.'

I glanced back at the lights of Schulau, now receding fast, and calculated the distance to the lights on the opposite shore. The river looked dark and oily, our wake a dirty grey. Patches of mist swirled low on the water. Away off our starboard beam, the steaming lights of a freighter winked through the murky gloom, and I almost wavered in my purpose. Then, I thought about Saturday night.

'All right, turn to starboard and head down-river,' I said.

Our wake curved sharply as he carried out the order and we ran with the following stream, our twin exhausts spitting and bobbling. Now, a head-wind was throwing back spray, which threatened to drench my new Burberry.

'This'll do, Parbs,' I said. 'Throw out the clutch, and let her idle.'

He did as he was told, and the bows sank down and she started to wallow. When I looked back the way we had come, I could just make out the lights of Schulau a good long way astern. I figured that, at this point, the Elbe must be two miles wide. Parbs turned round to face me.

'What now?'

'Into the cabin,' I said.

Mackenzie looked up. 'What's happening?'

'All right, Jock,' I said, 'nip along to the for'ard locker. You'll find some life-jackets there. Bring a couple, will you?'

'Sure.' He went to get the jackets, and when he brought them back, I nodded at Parbs and the woman.

'Get them on,' I said.

'No!' Parbs said. 'My wife cannot swim!'

'All the better, chum. You'll have to tow her, won't you? Should slow you down nicely,' I said.

Mackenzie glanced at the woman's scared face. 'We could just tie them up, instead . . .'

'We could, but we're not bloody going to – if you don't put them on, Parbs,' I said, 'I'll shove you overboard without them. So what's it going to be?'

Parbs looked at the pistol, then looked at his wife. 'First take your coat off,' he said.

The woman shrugged out of her duffel coat and her husband did the same, and we watched them tie on the bright yellow jackets. Parbs made one last appeal.

'Please . . . the river is dangerous . . .'

'Yes, and it's cold,' I said, 'but it isn't as cold as the Baltic.'

'We did not make that plan.'

'I don't give a chuff who made it – *out*!'

We herded them into the open stern and forced them over the side. The woman gasped loud as she hit the water, and started to thresh around, and I heard Parbs trying to calm her. They drifted away from the boat, and were soon swallowed up in the darkness.

'Will they make it?' Mackenzie said.

'Yes, they'll make it. You go below, and take care of Jagersberg.'

I tucked the pistol back into my waistband and laid a hand on the wheel and let in the clutch and opened the throttle. When we were under way, I turned our bows back to Schulau and put on maximum speed. We were back at the moorings in under ten minutes. I floated her in slow astern, and scrambled up on to the dock with the painter to warp her close alongside. Then I jumped back down to help Mackenzie bring out Jagersberg. We sat him on the boat-trailer, swathed in blankets. Although he was obviously still dazed, he seemed now to realize what was happening.

'Go get the car, Jock,' I said.

'Herr Stroud . . . Herr Stroud . . .'

'It's all right, Professor, we'll soon be on our way.'

'No, wait . . . you must listen . . . Ilse . . .'

I had almost forgotten the girl. 'Your daughter's safe, and you'll be seeing her shortly. We're picking her up on the way.'

He sighed. 'Thank God . . .'

I helped him to stand. 'Come on, now, here's the car.' As we sped east on Sülldorfer Landstrasse, 'Listen, Mackenzie,' I said, 'we can telephone Harvey from Suzi's place.'

'Good Lord! Yes, of course,' he said. 'I'd quite forgotten about the daughter!'

'You and me, both,' I said.

When we got to the house near Cuxhaven Allee I left them both in the car, and hurried upstairs and knocked on the door.

'Who is is?'

'It's me,' I said. 'Open up, Suzi – hurry!' She stood back as she opened the door. 'Is the girl all right?'

'Yes, we're about to start supper.'

'I'm afraid you'll be eating alone. I'm taking her with me right away, as soon as I've used your phone.'

The girl appeared in the sitting room doorway. '*Gott sie dank!*' she said. 'Herr Stroud – have you found my father?'

'Your father's outside, in the car. I've a call to make, then we're leaving.'

'Not so fast,' Suzi said. She grinned. 'Did you bring the rest of my money?'

I gave her the five hundred marks, and left her carefully counting the notes as I went in to use the phone. The switchboard at the airport hotel put me through to Harvey's room.

'Sam?'

'What's the score, old buddy?'

'Half an hour,' I said.

Later

Charlie had abandoned his crutches in favour of a walking stick, with whose rubber-tipped end he was poking at Jake.

'Hey – watch it, Charlie!' I said.

'It was wiping its snotty nose on my britches!'

'Come over here, Jake,' I said. 'Come away from the miserable bastard.'

'Jesus Christ,' he said, 'it's like a sodding menagerie.'

'Love me, love my dogs,' I said.

'Are we having a cup of tea, then?'

'Tea? It's half past six! I'm having a drink, mate. You please yourself.'

'I might have known,' he said. 'Got any bitter lemon?'

'No, just tonics,' I said.

'Orange squash?'

'Sorry.'

'Grapefruit?'

'No. I told you – just tonics,' I said.

'In that case, I'll have a cup of tea.'

'Oh, no, Charlie,' I said. 'You're a bloody nuisance – you know that?'

'Take your animals with you,' he said, 'and make us a sandwich while you're at it.'

'Smoked salmon do you?' I said.

The dogs loped after me, into the kitchen, and settled down on their beds. They knew where they weren't wanted. I put the kettle on, and opened up a tin of corned beef, and cut four thick slices of bread. I broke off from making the sandwiches to brew a pot of tea, then took the tray into the sitting room. Charlie was poking the fire.

'You're not supposed to do that in somebody else's house.'

'Who says so?'

'Old Yorkshire tradition.'

'Bullshit.'

'All right, poke away then,' I said.

'What's in the sandwiches?'

'*Pâté de fois.*'

'Pâté de what?'

'Corned beef.'

'That's better – why the hell didn't you say so?'

'Eat up, Charlie,' I said.

He poured himself tea, and picked up a sandwich. 'These all for me?' he said.

'Yes. I'll be going out for fish and chips later.'

'Any mustard?' he said.

I sloshed out an extra large Glenmorangie. 'Help yourself, Chas,' I said. 'Cupboard next to the Aga. You'll have to mix it, of course.'

'Mix it?'

'Yes, with water,' I said. 'You've got to smooth all the lumps out.'

'Lumps out?'

'Jesus! Listen,' I said, 'why don't you just eat your sandwich, and let's get down to it, eh?'

'All right, then – tell me about Mackenzie.'

'What about him?' I said.

'*I'm* asking *you.*'

'He's not a bad lad.'

'What's that supposed to mean?'

'It means just that,' I said. 'He'll do.'

I took a pull at the malt, and Charlie bit neatly into a sandwich. The dogs scratched soft on the door.

183

'What's that noise?' said Charlie.

'Must be mice,' I said. 'How's Professor Jagersberg?'

'I haven't a clue,' he said.

'Where is he, then? Have we still got him?'

'What do *you* care?' he said. 'You did the job, and that's all there is to it.'

'Do have more tea, Charles,' I said.

'You being sarcastic, Farrow?'

'Me? Of course not,' I said. 'Now . . . about my expenses . . .'

'What is it this time?' he said.

'Witherspoon's querying everything.'

'So?'

'I'm fed up with it, Charlie,' I said. 'I'm losing out on the bloody job!'

'Well, that's your fault,' he said. 'You shouldn't be such a big spender.'

'Big spender? Knackers!' I said.

'Language will get you nowhere. Jagersberg's gone,' he said.

'Don't change the sub— what? Where's he gone to?'

'Give you two guesses,' he said.

'You know something, Charlie? I don't want to know.'

'Why bother to ask, then?' he said. He started to eat his second sandwich. 'This is damned good bread.'

'Mrs Tidy bakes it.'

'Mrs who?' he said.

'Mrs Tidy. Tell me, Chas, what happened to Harvester?'

'I thought I'd told you; the Man kicked him out.'

'So what's he doing now, then?' I said.

'He works for the cousins, as a sort of consultant.'

'Marvellous,' I said. 'The bastard's probably making a fortune.'

'Incidentally,' he said, 'that official complaint is still being pursued.'

184

'Toomey?'

'Right,' he said.

'Toomey can go and get knotted.'

'Not the point,' Charlie said. 'You strained the special relationship.'

'Next time I see Toomey,' I said, 'I'll do a bloody sight more than just strain it.'

'Slow down, Farrow,' he said.

'All right, let's get back to my claim for expenses.'

'Any more corned beef?' he said.